THE PIRATE VILLAGE

Amy, Queen of the Pirates Ball

Judy Garwood

Amy, Queen of the Pirates Ball
This book is a work of fiction.
All names, characters, and events are fictitious.
Any references to real locales are used
fictitiously. Any resemblance to actual events or
persons, living or dead, is purely coincidental.

Print 978-1-71995-666-6

ACKNOWLEDGMENTS

I am truly grateful to my dear friend and Dominican sister, Kathy, who read every chapter as I wrote it and rewrote it!

To my son, Ben, who has always been supportive of my writing.

To Ray Taix, a photographer and artist who was born to create. Ray photographed the covers for *Mama, I'm Here* and *Amy, Queen of the Pirates Ball* and is the Illustrator of the incredible map of Pirates Village located on the first page of the book.

To my friends, and fellow Dominican sisters, Mary and Delia who offered me their hospitality.

And to Tara Kill, my patient editor at Wave Cloud.

I am grateful to the city of New Orleans where I grew up and especially the French Quarter where I spent many a Sunday afternoon exploring while my Mom joined her bridge group.

I am sure Jean Lafitte will forgive me for making him immortal but I do think I saw him last year on Mardi Gras Day, blending in with all the other pirates in the Quarter.

CONTENTS

CHAPTER ONE
Amy's Return

Marie Savion stood alone on the dock. She turned up the collar on her coat but it gave little protection from the rain and heavy fog over the ocean. Removing her glasses she wiped the rain from the lens. With her glasses off her eyes were plain and gentle but with them on the rims pressed against her dark eyebrows made her appear proper and very strict. Traveling to the island and returning to the mainland would be impossible unless the ferry appeared soon. She cringed as waves lashed out against the decaying underlying timbers, making the pier sway.

She had been sent to bring Amy, a special young girl who lived at the orphanage on the island, to New Orleans. If she did not bring Amy back in time, the curse would come to pass and the city to which they would be returning would find its final resting place at the bottom of the Mississippi River. Only Amy could save the French Quarter from disaster. And according to the curse, Amy had to do that before she turned nineteen in two weeks. It was already the end of January. They had little time to waste.

It was just a few days ago that she left New Orleans, arriving in London just in time to catch a train to a small village on the west coast of Scotland. Unfortunately she missed the last ferry to the island. She spent the night at The Black Swan, a local Inn and Tavern. A roaring fire and a delicious lamb pie restored her good spirits.

But the weather was not cooperating this morning. She would be late arriving at St. Luke's Orphanage. It made her uneasy to know she was traveling only hours ahead of a storm with strong winds and punishing rain but nothing would stop her from completing her task.

Marie thought about the orphanage, the place Amy had resided for the past thirteen years, since she had been rescued from a sinking pleasure cruise at the age of five. Unfortunately her parents, as well as all the adults on the ship, were reported as drowned. Marie had read that over one hundred years ago the orphanage was started as a refuge for children whose parents, many working on fishing boats, were left orphaned when their parents were lost at sea.

Marie had served as a Nanny for the Claiborne family since Lily Claiborne and her younger sister, Celeste, were babies. Marie was just as devastated as Lily when Celeste, at the age of eighteen, ran off with a young man she'd met during Mardi Gras. Celeste left a note saying she was going to travel the world with Philippe. No last name and no more information.

Celeste running off took everyone by surprise, most of all her elderly parents. In their frustration they blamed the nanny, Marie, and fired her on the spot. From that moment on Lily had given up her freedom and any life she might have had to take care of her parents.

It was only after her parents died that Lily brought back Marie, who was now married, to manage the family home in the French Quarter. Marie's husband, Marcel, took over the duties of driving the cars and tending the lush gardens that filled the courtyard which pleased Lily since she would now have fewer responsibilities in the upkeep of the large house.

A few years after Celeste left, Lily received a postcard from London. Celeste said she had given birth, on a lovely February afternoon, to Amy, a beautiful baby girl.

Lily tried to find Celeste but she disappeared once again. Even so Lily was overjoyed to know that the curse had been averted with the birth of Amy.

They spent the next eighteen years looking for them in vain. They seemed to be one step behind Celeste and her beautiful daughter. Lily found a marriage certificate for Celeste and Philippe during their brief stay in Paris.

A few weeks earlier Lily saw a TV documentary about St. Luke's Orphanage and knew at once the young woman playing in the courtyard was her missing niece. The young girl was the very image of her younger sister, Celeste.

She knew for sure when she tracked down the show's producer who told her that Amy was eighteen years old. Little else was known about her past other than she had been rescued by a fisherman thirteen years ago clinging to debris in the Irish Sea. The name, Amy, was marked on a label in her sweater.

Debilitated by a severe flu, Lily sent Marie to bring the girl home.

Out on the frothy whitecaps a light flashed, then disappeared. On one hand Marie was relieved that the ferry was in sight but, with a sense of horror, she realized the flashing light was fixed to the bow of a tiny boat that looked out of control and heading straight for the dock.

From the fog a figure dressed in a yellow rain slicker leaped onto the dock and secured the lines. His face was hidden by a broad brimmed yellow rain hat tied tightly under his chin.

"Cutter's Island?"

"Yes. St. Luke's Orphanage."

He said something she couldn't hear above the howling wind then he seized her around the waist and unceremoniously dropped her into the well of the boat.

After treacherous waves lifted and dropped the boat behind walls of water they finally pulled up to a concrete jetty.

The boatman helped her up and yelled into her ear. "Stone stairs at the end of the dock...follow the path through the woods. It takes ye right to the door of St. Luke's. Call me when ye want to come back. Be quick. There's a nice bit o' wind gettin' up."

He deposited her on the slippery dock and set a small valise next to her. With a quick wave he was gone.

Sleet stung her cheeks. She picked up her bag and carefully made her way up the moss covered stairs.

Following the path through the trees she emerged in front of a massive, three story, dark grey stone mansion.

A tall, slim woman stood in the doorway and beckoned her to hurry inside.

"Mrs. Johnston? I'm Marie Savion."

"Yes, yes. I saw the ferry. I've been expecting you. Hang your raincoat and hat here."

Marie's rain gear joined a collection of other coats in the entryway.

Mrs. Johnston led the way into an office to the left of the front door. A huge stone fireplace was ablaze with light and warmth. Jewel toned Persian rugs covered the aged wood floors. Two comfortable-looking sofas and several overstuffed chairs were scattered around the large room. A huge mahogany desk with two Chippendale chairs for guest seating and a massive bookcase behind it, was at the far end of the room.

Marie sat in one of the chairs while Mrs. Johnston resumed her place at the desk. Retrieving a file folder from her bag Marie placed it on the desk.

Mrs. Johnston spent a few minutes looking through the paperwork. She knew it would be in order. For the past two weeks she had been in contact with Amy's aunt in New Orleans. Miss Claiborne had faxed, emailed, and Fed Ex'd everything she needed to prove Amy was born on February 12, 1993 in London to Celeste Claiborne, a single mother who listed her home as 426 Royal Street, New Orleans, Louisiana. Miss Claiborne had also told her a little about the family home in the French Quarter where Amy would soon be living.

A week earlier Mrs. Johnston had received pictures of Celeste Claiborne. She agreed Amy was the image of her mother. "It appears all is in order."

"Mrs. Johnston, was there anything Amy especially liked doing here at the orphanage?" Their cook, taking a liking to the girl, let her help out in the kitchen preparing meals, but with almost disastrous results. "Well...she wanted to help out in the kitchen but...she loves to daydream and not paying attention she constantly substituted salt for sugar."

Amy's other substitutions were even worse, Mrs. Johnston thought, leaving out the part where the other strange combinations sent everyone running from the main dining room. The cook finally banned her from the kitchen. "She loves to read and gardening is a hobby of hers." She was relieved that someone had come for the high spirited young girl. It was now January. Amy would be nineteen years old next month and overdue to go off on her own. Being a daydreamer left her ill prepared to face the working world.

Marie noticed a photograph of Celeste that lay on Mrs. Johnston's desk.

"Have you been with the family for very long?"

"Yes. Since Celeste, Amy's mother, and her sister, Lily, were very young."

Mrs. Johnston picked up the photograph and handed it to Marie. "She might like to have this." The resemblance to her mother was unmistakable. "I have seen many pictures provided by her Aunt. As you know I've been in touch with Miss Claiborne for the past two weeks. It's good to have a last name for her and a caring Aunt who wants her to come live with her in New Orleans."

"You told Miss Lily a fisherman found Amy. I would love to thank him, if I can."

"Seamus, the man who now runs the ferryboat found Amy. He was a fisherman in those days. He brought Amy to us. When she arrived she was in and out of consciousness."

"I see."

"She was only five years old and has little memory of what happened. She has never spoken of it."

Marie checked her watch. "I don't mean to rush but there is a storm coming and I have to get back to the

Mainland. I was very fortunate to get the last two sleeping berths on the midnight train to London. I was told if we miss this train it will be days before sleeping berths are available."

"In that case come with me and we will find Amy. I have an idea she's in the Library. Your coming is not a surprise, although she expected you yesterday. She is excited about her new home. She speaks of nothing else. She's read every book we have about New Orleans and the French Quarter. She loves especially loves tales about pirates and sorcery.

Amy was standing at the window in the spacious Library. She had seen the ferry boat and wondered why Seamus would come out on such a dreadful night. It must be her Aunt come to take her to America.

This was her favorite room. It was filled with books that took her to wonderful places. Sitting by the window, and looking out at the sea, she imagined she was part of the crew on Blackbeard's pirate ship. And sometimes she wrapped herself in one of the long green velvet drapes flanking the many windows in the room and pretended she was Scarlet O'Hara.

Amy lightly brushed her fingers over the leather bound books. Did her Mother love to read, too, she wondered?

Trying as hard as she could, she remembered very little about the last time she saw her Mother. It had been a festive night aboard a big ship. It had been her fifth birthday. A very loud alarm sounded. There was confusion. People rushing around.

But she could still remember her Mother saying to her "Be my brave little girl, Amy."

Then the boat, with Amy and all the other crying children, was quickly lowered into the sea and disappeared in the swell of a wave and a blanket of fog that enveloped the sinking ship.

"Amy...Amy...you have a visitor." Daydreaming as usual Mrs. Johnston thought.

Amy turned, surprised to find the elderly lady standing in the doorway with a stern look on her face. A woman she'd never seen before was standing beside Mrs. Johnston with an amused smile on her face.

The two women entered the Library.

"I have some good news for you. This is Miss Savion and she has been sent here by your aunt, Miss Lily Claiborne, to take you to the family home in New Orleans. We spoke of this, remember? Your aunt, saw you on the TV show that filmed here. You are going to the French Quarter home where your Aunt Lily and your Mother grew up."

"My Mother! You've found my Mother?"

Marie spoke quickly. "No, we haven't. But your Aunt Lily has not stopped looking for her the past twenty years... ever since your Mother left home."

Looking at Amy, Marie thought she could be Celeste standing there. Silky black hair in one thick braid fell over her shoulder. Her skin was fair in contrast and her eyes were black as night and as bright as the stars.

Mrs. Johnston sat in one of the wing chairs and indicated to Marie and Amy to also sit down, hoping a little conversation would help.

"Amy, your Aunt told me a little about the family home in the New Orleans French Quarter. The house is very old.

It was built in the early 1800's. The pirate Jean Lafitte visited there quite often, your aunt told me—"

"---In the house? I've read about the famous pirate Jean Lafitte. He visited someone in the house?"

Marie was thrilled to see Amy smile.

"Yes. He did. He had a...friend...who worked in the house. I have much to tell you but we have a train to catch."

"My dear, why don't you select a bag from the closet and do pack with haste."

Amy rushed out of the Library almost colliding with three young children who had gathered, waiting to see what was going on. She talked to them as she opened the door to the luggage room and picked out a carpet bag that she knew would hold her few treasures and fewer clothes, all she had in the world that were hers.

They had a million questions that she didn't have answers for. All she could tell them was that this was the person who had come to take her to America.

A tear slid unnoticed down her face. She was leaving the only family she had to go to a new world.

After saying goodbye to everyone and waving to Mrs. Johnston Amy followed Marie down the stone stairs to the ferryboat bobbing up and down in the choppy waves.

Seamus helped Amy into the boat yelling to be heard above the roaring wind. "Brought the other lady over a bit ago. Going for a cup o' tea in the village, are ye, Miss Amy?"

"No. Seamus." Amy giggled. "This is Miss Marie. She's come to take me to my Aunt's home in New Orleans,

Louisiana...in the French Quarter. It sounds beautiful, doesn't it?"

"Aye, it does. Blessed journey to ye both."

Nothing more was said since the wind and waves made their own loud music, blocking out all conversation. That was fine with Marie who worried about Amy telling everyone their personal business. As soon as they were alone she would have a talk with the young girl.

When they were finally standing on the unsteady dock Marie turned to Seamus still in the boat securing the lines. "I want to thank you for saving Amy that night."

"It was a miracle, it was. I was out fishing that night and found her, just a little one she was, clinging to the top of an old sea boat. I brought her to St. Luke's."

Amy had a thoughtful look on her face. A brief memory, just that minute, flashed through her mind. "What happened to the other man?"

Seamus stopped and leaped onto the dock beside them. "Naw, ye was alone."

"No. I remember now a man put me on top of the boat. He was holding a rope. He helped you get me into your fishing boat. I remember you were very happy to see him."

"Ye be mistaken. Now I have to secure me boat. We're in for a spell of bad weather so ye best hurry if ye're to catch that train."

They turned and waved at him as Marie checked her watch again and hurried off.

He smiled and waved in return.

After all these years Seamus had hoped she would never remember what had happened that night, that

10

there was a man in the water, a man that Seamus had rescued and then kept hidden for thirteen years. All those years watching, waiting and hoping that this would never happen. But now there were going to be consequences.

Marie placed their tickets in the outstretched hand of an elderly steward. They were all crowded inside the tiny entry platform. The train whistle blew and jolted to a start.

"Follow me." The steward pointed out the cabins and handed Marie two keys.

"Anything you need, just push the call button. Tea is served in the dining car." He indicated the adjoining carriage, adjusted his train cap and hurried away to assist passengers that were milling about in the narrow corridor.

Marie opened the door labeled with a brass number six and handed the key to Amy.

It was small but with room for whatever was needed for the night. The day sofa had been turned down into an inviting bed with soft pillows and crisp white linen sheets and a warm blanket.

"I'm just next door. It's late but maybe they will have more than tea...some sandwiches would be nice." Marie left Amy to explore on her own.

A door to a tiny bathroom was only steps from the bed. There was a built in desk with a chair in the corner. Finishing her exploration of the first train cabin she'd ever been in she locked the door behind her.

She joined Marie and they quickly made their way down the passageway to the dining car. Rain beat against the window beside their small table so the only light was a tiny lamp that threw a golden glow over everything.

Chippendale style dining chairs seated four comfortably. Many were occupied by only two travelers.

They were delighted when a waiter brought a plate of tiny sandwiches and biscuits with their tea.

Amy could tell Marie was tired, having done so much in one day, so she suggested they retire. They could talk the next day. Marie was more than agreeable to the idea.

When the train came to a stop, with the sound of metal grinding on metal, in London the next morning Amy was still awake not wanting to miss seeing the charming small villages and wide open moors that flashed by the large window in her small room.

The elderly steward she met the night before knocked on her door delivering a tray with hot tea and sweet biscuits. He called out "We're in Paddington Station."

She dressed quickly and was waiting in the hallway when Marie joined her in a big of a rush.

Marie had the proper passport and all necessary papers she needed to get Amy onto the plane and on their way to New Orleans, Louisiana.

They had little time to talk after they arrived at Heathrow. Once they boarded the plane Amy gripped the seat the minute they were in the air.

Once safely airborne she fell into a deep sleep. Marie thought it was best that she did sleep since they encountered rough air over the ocean and she knew Amy would not be at ease.

The turbulence was especially bad as they landed at the New Orleans International Airport. They were told to expect the weather to be cold, humid and raining. Not a rare combination but unpleasant all the same.

A man was waiting for them when they arrived. Marie hugged him briefly and introduced him as Marcel, her husband. Marie told her that Marcel was not only the driver but he tended the garden, too.

Amy thought back about the place she'd spent the last thirteen years. At the orphanage she had helped the cook but the times she enjoyed the most was when she was working in the garden. They grew their own vegetables and harvested the fruit trees.

They had chickens for eggs and goats for milk and cheese. Sadly, she had found it very difficult to eat goat stew. She kept naming the goats and strongly contested their demise. Finally the cook relented and more chickens disappeared than goats.

Marie sat next to Marcel in the front so Amy had the entire back seat to herself.

Wide avenues, huge trees, and colorfully painted houses flashed by on their way to 426 Royal Street, the home where her Mother had grown up. Amy was beside herself with excitement.

The European houses she had read about were much like the ones she was seeing now, narrow with ornate wrought iron balconies over the street. Here and there she caught a glimpse, through an open gate, of lush, flower filled courtyards.

"I can't wait to meet my Aunt Lily."

"You will not see her until after dinner. She's been a bit ill but not to worry. In the meantime you can explore the house. We have a Library just as big as the one at St. Luke's."

Marie turned to find Amy looking out her window. "Amy, that street is called Pirates Alley. There were many cafes and taverns here in the 1700's where the pirates congregated.

Marcel turned the car towards Decatur then took a left to follow the Mississippi River. Amy noticed a fast moving dark grey cloud. "Marie, look there's a storm headed this way."

At that moment the skies turned dark, rain beat down a rhythm on the roof of the car and lightning flashed around them.

Marie gave Marcel a sideways glance and clutched his arm. "There's a saying in New Orleans...wait and the weather will change."

Serena wanted to see Amy, the child of her only son. She lifted her face to the rain. With a snap of her fingers and a twist of her wrist the skies cleared and the sun came out.

Serena knew the girl had seen her. Only Philippe's child could see her on this side of the wall. A warmth touched her eyes. A part of her son was alive with Amy. She smiled, something she hadn't done in many years.

"Did you see that?" Amy felt faint.

"See what?"

"There was a...a black carriage...and...and...a woman dress in black lace was driving four black horses and...it was floating in the air." Amy stuttered in disbelief.

"Ah...that was Serena. They call her The Black Witch." Marie turned to Marcel. "So like her father, isn't she?" Turning in her seat she advised Amy in a serious tone of voice. "Definitely do not mention this to your Aunt. We have to get to the house right now but I promise tonight I will come to your room and tell you everything. And look, the sun is out."

The Black Witch! Amy quietly clapped her hands together. She was going to love living in this strange and wonderful place.

CHAPTER TWO
A Secret Door

If Amy thought St. Luke's Orphanage, built in the early 1800's, was the most beautiful mansion she could ever imagine she was wrong.

Marcel pulled into a covered area off the street. "Miss Amy, this is called a Porte- Cochere. In the 1800's guests stepped from their horse drawn carriages to enter the house, sheltered from bad weather."

"Thank you, Marcel. I have read about such places."

She decided to enter the house by walking through a courtyard with a three tiered fountain in the middle made of copper aged green. Each bowl was held up underneath by three carved cherubs.

Tall palms, majestic Magnolia trees, lush ferns, towering pure white Bird of Paradise with fragrant gardenias, jasmine and roses filled every space in the garden. It must have been what Eden looked like, Amy thought.

There were teak weathered-to-grey benches and comfortable lounge chairs for sitting and reading.

From the street the house looked unassuming but once through the carriage park it opened into an enormous three story mansion surrounded by twelve foot stone walls. The main entrance to the house faced the courtyard.

Marie led her inside. Amy didn't look at the one hundred year old heart of pine floors or the Chippendale dining room table and chairs. She missed the huge gleaming Mahogany glass fronted china cabinet filled with a gold rimmed dinner service fit for a Queen. She didn't think for a second about the sparkling Austrian crystals that hung from magnificent chandeliers in every room. Instead she noticed the wonderful brocade upholstered wing chairs placed, here and there, ever so close to windows where one could sit for hours and read.

"When can I meet my Aunt Lily?"

"Maybe later." Maybe not, Marie thought, hoping Lily would be in a better mood than when she left to find her niece. "Why don't I show you around?"

Amy followed Marie down a long hallway. Marie opened a large door that opened to a huge room with fifteen foot ceilings. Every wall was lined with mahogany bookcases filled with leather bound editions of the classics. Amy ran her fingers over books by Tennessee Williams, Faulkner, Flannery O'Connor, John Steinbeck and many other writers that she recognized at once.

There was a magnificent fireplace with an ornate hand carved wood mantel. A fire had been lit giving the room a warm feeling against the cold rainy day.

"Marie, I have forgotten my Mother's face." Her voice was but a whisper. "I can only remember her voice. When I close my eyes I hear her telling me to be brave, that she will come for me one day. Will I forget her voice as well?"

"No, Cher. I believe your Mother is but only lost right now. I have often felt her in these rooms. I know one day and she will come home to find you and you will remember her at that moment. A child never forgets her Mother."

Amy's face radiated a glow of hope.

A beautiful wing chair caught her attention. Amy briefly wondered why such a lovely chair was facing the wall. She turned the chair around and sat down. She could feel her Mother all around her.

"This will be my favorite chair."

Marie smiled. "Your Mother loved that chair."

Although choosing her mother's favorite chair touched Amy's heart, at the same time it was crushingly sad to think she'd never have a chance to share those things with her.

"Your Mother loved to read and she wrote stories when she was a young child."

Amy ran her fingers over some of the books and wondered if her Mother had touched the very same books.

Marie sensing Amy's returning sadness spoke quickly.

"Let's go choose your bedroom."

Marie started up the huge main staircase with Amy close behind her.

"Choose?" Amy laughed. "There are so many?"

"There are ten bedrooms all with their own baths. Your Aunt has her own bedroom and bath on the first floor. The stairs are too much for her now. "

"I am sorry to hear that. I could read to her. I used to do that for the younger children when they were sick."

"We'll see." Marie was not going to be the one to tell Amy that Lily hated reading, hating daydreaming, hated anything that her sister Celeste had loved so much. Being left with the responsibility of taking care of her elderly parents, and giving up her freedom to do so, made Lily Claiborne a bitter woman. Lily had vented her anger by turning all of her sister's favorite chairs to face the walls and removed any picture of her sister from the rooms. Marie wondered what she was going to do with a young woman who looked so much like Celeste.

"There are six bedrooms on the second floor and the staff has three bedrooms on the third floor. Marcel and I live above the carriage house where all the cars are stored."

"Carriage houses. I have read of such things. They held the carriages used in the 1800's."

"There are still carriages in the French Quarter."

"You mean like the—"

Marie's turned with a finger to her lips. She spoke in a whisper, "Remember...not a word to your Aunt Lily about that other thing when you see her. We will speak later." Marie continued up the massive staircase. "The carriages I'm referring to are the ones that take tourists around the French Quarter."

"I shall do that, too, then. There are so many things to discover."

"Yes."

"You said the staff have rooms on the third floor. Who are they?

"Melita is the cook and Gloria is the housekeeper."

"I used to help the cook at St. Luke's. Maybe I could help Melita."

Marie steered her in another direction. "Maybe you'd like to help Marcel take care of the gardens. Oh, in case I forget to tell you, my cousin Jimmy may pay you a visit.

He's very sweet and will be happy to show you around the French Quarter."

"Oh yes, thank you. I would love to have a new friend."

Marie led the way down a dimly lit hallway to a door at the very end. Amy almost swooned as she rushed past her into the room.

The glow from the firelight gave the delicate rose painted walls a soft feeling. Pale rose silk brocade hangings surrounded a huge four-poster bed. She restrained an urge to jump atop the tapestry bedspread.

A small overstuffed chair was placed beside the fireplace and near the one window.

Amy whirled. "This is the one. I love this room, Marie. Can I choose this room?"

"Ma, Petite, you can most definitely have this room. You can have any room on this floor. In the 1800s this room was used for storage. Later your Mother claimed this room as her own. This became her bedroom."

"I knew it, Marie. I can feel her presence right now. Just as I know the chair beside the fireplace was her favorite place to sit and read."

Amy shook off the sadness. How could she be sad when right now she felt closer to her Mother than she had ever felt? Every dream she had for the last thirteen years would come true, she was positive of that.

"And someone lit a fire. How wonderful! Is it cold in the French Quarter all year long?"

"Only a short time in the winter but when it is cold it is very cold."

Amy smiled. "Will you tell me all about the French Quarter? And does it snow in the winter?"

Marie laughed. "So many questions. I have to oversee dinner. Why don't you unpack? I'll be back later."

Closing the door behind her Marie hurried downstairs.

Amy clapped her hands and danced around the room. She almost collided with a stout little fellow who stood leaning against the wall. He had shocking red hair that stuck up in the back. He wore a tiny green paisley vest and dark red velvet knee pants with green and white checkered socks and shiny black shoes with buckles. He was watching her with an amused smile on his face.

"Who are you?" Amy demanded terrified and curious at the same time.

"Hello to you, too. I'm Jimmy O'Brien."

"Marie told me you would visit. But tell me, Jimmy O'Brien, were you hiding in the room before I came in?"

"Oh, no, I never hide."

"I know! I know!" Amy was thrilled with an idea. "You waved a magic wand and...poof...you appeared!"

"Exactly!"

"Really?" Amy was astounded.

"No! NOT really!" He laughed. "I came through a secret door next to the fireplace."

Amy stood with a hand on her hip. "Will you show me this secret door?"

"Of course."

Jimmy pushed a brick over the fireplace mantel and a concealed door opened.

Amy rushed over and stuck her head into the void. "There's a winding passageway—"

Someone groaned loudly nearby and it wasn't Jimmy. Amy jumped back into the room to find Marie standing in the doorway with a stern look on her face directed at Amy's new friend.

"Jimmy, didn't I tell you not tonight."

"Marie, Jimmy is showing me such wonderful things about the house like a secret door!"

"Really." Marie smiled. "Dinner now. Jimmy...lock the door on your way out."

"All right. All right. I'm going. Amy, if you like, I will see you tomorrow and show you the sights, as they say."

"Thank you, Jimmy. I look forward to tomorrow...." She watched her new friend disappear through the secret door and heard a click. Amy thought she might do a little exploring on her own later so she was a bit disappointed that he had locked the door behind him.

"You know, Amy, there are many secret panels in the house that lead to small rooms and furniture with secret drawers."

"How exciting! Will you show me sometime?"

"Of course. But now we are going to dinner."

She followed Marie down the stairs in great anticipation of meeting her Aunt.

A wonderful aroma of baked chicken permeated the dining room. Amy sat in a dining chair and looked around the room. "Is that my Aunt?" She pointed to an oil painting in a prominent place in the dining room right over an antique marble topped sideboard that dominated one wall.

"Yes. It is."

The woman in the portrait was dressed all in dark grey, seated in what looked like a very uncomfortable chair and had a stern look on her face. Even Mrs. Richardson hadn't looked like that after Amy had accidentally committed the most gravest of errors in the kitchen.

"Your Aunt will not be at dinner but she asks if you would come to her room later."

"Will you go with me?"

"Of course."

Amy almost sighed in relief. She hoped her Aunt would not look as stern as she seemed in the picture.

At that moment a very jovial woman entered the room carrying a huge silver platter filled with silver domed dishes. A small woman was right behind her toting a smaller tray with various condiment bowls.

"This is Melita our wonderful cook and I told you about Glory, her kitchen assistant and mostly the housekeeper."

"Everything smells wonderful!"

"Miss Amy, welcome home." They said in unison.

The cook placed the heavy platter on the sideboard. Glory placed her tray next to it.

Before Melita had a chance to serve her Amy jumped up. "I can serve myself. Thank you. I know I shall love everything."

Melita, with Glory hurrying behind her, left the room.

"Marie, where is Marcel? Does he not eat dinner with us?"

"He had errands to run for your Aunt. He'll eat dinner later. Do not worry yourself, ma petite."

"I've never seen chicken cooked like this." Amy was poking at the chicken on the platter.

"It's a New Orleans dish. It's called smothered chicken over rice."

"It smells...interesting." Not wanting to offend anyone Amy hastened to add, "I'm quite used to different food but I'm sure this will become my favorite."

Amy served herself a huge helping of every item. Marie smiled. Amy ate with as much gusto as her Mother used to. If they had found Amy maybe there was a chance Celeste was still alive. She had often thought so. She could feel Celeste's presence somewhere out there.

"Please tell me all about Jimmy. Does he live on the third floor?"

Marie laughed. "Oh no. Your Aunt would be furious if she knew he was even in the house. It would be better not to mention his visit to your aunt when you see her. Also not a word about the other person you saw...okay?" Marie put her finger to her lips.

"Okay. But you promised to tell me all about that...person with the flying carriage." Amy changed the subject because it seemed to cause Marie great concern. "I think Jimmy's ever so sweet and you said he's your cousin, right? Where does he live?"

Marie wanted to delay answering the first question for a while. "Jimmy lives in Leprechaun City."

"Where is that?"

"Below the streets of the French Quarter."

"There's a Leprechaun City below the street?"

"It's not exactly a whole city. Jimmy just calls it that. There already was a tunnel. Jimmy and his brothers extended out the tunnel and built a house for themselves."

"How exciting! Do you think he would he give me a tour?"

"Ask him."

"I've read about Leprechauns...I've never actually seen one until now and—"

Nothing more was said since Melita and Glory returned bringing new trays laden with many good things to eat and Amy was very hungry.

When the sideboard looked like it couldn't hold one more platter Amy finally stopped eating.

She had consumed plump portions of smothered chicken, rice, peas and lettuce braised in butter, which was very English, and southern banana pudding for dessert.

Amy thanked the staff and told them she never ate with such an appetite but she really hadn't had much to eat for a few days.

Marie checked her watch. "It's still a bit early to meet your aunt Lily. Would you like see the Conservatory?"

"Oh, yes, please!" Amy was very excited. This was the house her mother had grown up in, the bedroom was one her mother had slept in. The Library where she had sat on rainy days reading the many books. And she was sure the Conservatory would be filled with roses and gardenias as those were the flowers she imaged her Mother lovingly tending the most.

"There are so many rooms! But, Marie, don't we have to take our dishes into the kitchen?"

"Glory will do that for us. Follow me."

The dining room opened to a large glass room that was surprisingly bare of any flowers. The only furniture was a massive sideboard, a game table and four chairs. There was also an overstuffed chair and a floor lamp. The room was barely furnished.

Amy looked around in dismay. "I thought there would be lots of roses and wonderful exotic orchards and things. Where are all the flowers?"

"Your Mother loved flowers. When she was here the entire room was filled with white flowers of all kinds. Especially white Bird of Paradise. There were containers filled with white tulips and white azaleas and gardenias. When she left your Aunt eventually cleared out every container in this room. It was a very sad time."

"I see." Amy wondered if she would ever understand her Aunt. How could Amy love someone who would take away such beauty and joy?

"But you are here now. How would you like to bring your Mother's garden back?"

"Oh, I would." Amy was filled with joy. "More than anything. We'll work together to make it just as it was."

"And I will help you, ma petite. This house also belongs to you now as much as it does your Aunt Lily, just as your Mother would have wished."

"I am sure my Aunt will be delighted with what we plan to do."

Marie knew that Lily would hate any changes especially any that her sister had loved. She walked over to a mahogany sideboard. A marble top held bits of mail. She reached around behind the massive piece of furniture and a small compartment on the back opened.

"I have something to show you. Your Aunt Lily put away all the pictures of your mother after she called to tell us about your birth but I saved many in a photo album. I hoped one day we would find you and you would want to see them, to see what she looked like when she was young."

Amy looked up with tears in her eyes. "I do. Thank you. I can feel her all around me. I know she will return one day."

Amy held the book to her heart. Then Marie pulled up a chair beside hers and they opened the album together.

Marie told her many stories about her Mother's life in the house. Amy laughed when she heard about the wonderful times her Mother had here.

Amy realized it was getting late. She shut the book and Marie put it back.

"I will retrieve it later. It is yours to keep. Now, are you ready to meet your Aunt Lily?"

"Oh, yes, please!"

"Don't expect much for now...she's been a bit under the weather." Marie thought to herself that Lily was disagreeable all the time.

Amy followed Marie down a long hallway passing the Library and the Morning Room, as Marie called it, to a room on the very end. She tapped on the door.

"Don't be tiresome, Marie. Come in." A gruff voice shouted from inside the room.

Marie walked in with Amy huddled behind her.

"Where is that child?" Lily's voice boomed out.

Marie moved aside and Amy looked right at the most unpleasant looking woman she'd ever seen. Her white hair was in a horrible disarray. She was wearing a flannel nightgown the color of mildew, Amy thought. And by the volume of her voice it didn't sound like she was one bit under the weather at all.

Her aunt was propped up in a huge four poster bed by pillows in various shades of purple velvet. Gold silk drapes were held back by turquoise and blue tie backs. Everything looked very festive except for the terrible scowl on her aunt's face. She looked like she'd just eaten something that was very disagreeable indeed.

"I want to...to thank you, aunt...for bringing me here." Amy stuttered and she hardly ever stuttered.

"Oh, stop groveling. If it hadn't been for that blasted curse I would have left you to rot where you were." Her aunt studied her like a bug under glass. "You look like her."

"Curse?"

"Ah, I see Marie has not told you anything. What are you waiting for, Marie? There's not much time left." She waved her hand in a dismissive gesture.

"Do you think I might visit again...tomorrow?" "Marie, why did you get back so late from the airport?

"You made the flight arrangements so you know we came directly here."

"I know everything. Just making sure you know that." "Aunt Lily, until tomorrow?"

"No! Marie will let you know if I want to see you and when. Now get out of my room. I want to sleep."

Amy had to stop herself from bowing and walking backwards out of the room. This was not what she expected, she thought. She had been hoping her aunt would welcome her into the family. Maybe her aunt would see things differently if she prevented the curse from happening.

Amy waited while Marie retrieved the photo album. They went upstairs together.

Amy sat on her bed. Her hands never left the leather photo album by her side.

Marie took the small chair by the fire.

"Please tell me all about this curse and the part I am to play in it."

"You saw The Black Witch, on our way to the house. Her name is Serena and she put a curse on the Claiborne family in the early 1800s because of the pirate, Jean Lafitte."

"Tell me what happened. What was the connection between the Black Witch and Jean Lafitte?"

"They were in love. Serena was a beautiful girl. She lived in this very same house and worked for the Claiborne family. That's how she met Jean Lafitte. He came to the Claiborne house on an important matter but there was great animosity between Lafitte and Governor Claiborne. Lafitte saw her and fell instantly in love. They met in secret places. There was a rumor that she was going to have his baby. When Mrs. Claiborne found out she sent the girl into the street with only the clothes she was wearing. Jean Lafitte was away at sea and knew nothing of what was happening. The young girl disappeared but years later she returned as the Black Witch, no longer a sweet young girl but a woman to be reckoned with."

"Is she really a witch? Was she born a witch?"

"Yes and she has a brother who is the Warlock of the City. He has quite a large following."

"What about her baby?"

"Serena returned with a son. She put a curse on the Claiborne family. They had to provide a beautiful girl, before she turns nineteen years of age, to be The Pirate Queen at a Ball during Mardi Gras. Each generation has abided by the curse. It is not so easy to guarantee a Claiborne child will be a girl or beautiful. Because from that moment on the Claiborne's produced mostly boys.

"My Mother is very beautiful."

"Yes. Your grandmother called your Aunt Lily an ugly old maid and said at least they had one beautiful daughter, your mother. Then your mother did something so unexpected...she ran away before she reigned as Queen."

"Aunt Lily must have been disappointed not having a Mardi Gras Queen in the family."

Marie smiled. She didn't want to tell Amy that her Aunt Lily had been relieved that she didn't have to bow to her sister at the Pirates Ball. Lily hated Celeste because she was everything Lily wasn't, she was popular and beautiful. Everyone loved Celeste, except Lily.

"Your Mother sent a postcard to your aunt when you were born in London, which was a great relief, because the family would now have a Pirate Queen to satisfy the curse, but before your aunt could find her she disappeared again.

You were destined to be the Pirate Queen. But no one knew where your mother had taken you. If you were not found before you turned nineteen years of age then the curse would come to pass and the French Quarter would sink beneath the waves of the Mississippi River, along with the Claiborne family home. It was very important that you were found."

"But I'll be nineteen very soon."

"Yes, the day after Mardi Gras. If it hadn't been for the curse your aunt would have left you in that Orphanage."

"Then if, in her mind, I am fulfilling the conditions of the curse why doesn't my aunt want me here?"

"She gave up her life to take care of her parents when your mother ran away with that boy. After that, no one was allowed to speak her name. Lily promised her Mother on her deathbed that she would find Celeste and bring her home.

"When I was at the orphanage I used to wish for my Mother to come for me. I know she's alive somewhere. I often see her in my dreams."

"I do, too. Your parents are very special. I knew for sure that you were, too, when you saw the Black Witch. And you are the image of your Mother. That makes your aunt angry when she sees you. It makes her remember what your mother did."

"Tell me about the Pirates Ball, and being Pirate Queen, and Mardi Gras. I did read something about the famous Mardi Gras it in the library at St. Luke's."

"I am truly exhausted and need to get a good night's sleep. Jimmy will tell you everything you need to know."

"Thank you, Marie...for bringing me home."

Marie smiled. "When you wake up, pull the brocade sash next to the bed against the wall. Glory will bring you a surprise. Then wait in your room for me."

"I will!" Amy was intrigued but there were so many questions she wanted to ask.

She carefully placed the leather photo album under her mattress. In the orphanage she had always put things of great value under her mattress knowing that was a very safe place.

She slipped on a soft nightgown that had been provided for her and climbed under a light feather comforter.

Marie hurried down the stairs. She left before Amy could ask her more questions. How could she explain that Jimmy was hundreds of years old and would show her things and places she wouldn't find in all the books in the library.

CHAPTER THREE
Exploring Treasure Island

Amy woke to sun pouring into the room. She lay under the soft down comforter and thought about how her life had changed. Just a few days ago she was sleeping in a small room at the Orphanage with only the books in the library to keep her company. Now she was in an exciting place where someone called the Black Witch drove a carriage pulled by four horses ten feet above the street. This was truly a place of magic. A place where what she imagined might come true. Amy stretched, threw the covers back and was surprised to see her clothes washed, ironed and neatly folded and placed on the small chair just inside the door.

Remembering what Marie had said she pulled the brocade sash beside the bed. While she was waiting she changed into her newly cleaned jeans, t-shirt, sweatshirt and tennis shoes.

There was a soft knock on the door. Amy opened the door and Glory entered carrying a tray filled with domed silver plates that she placed on a table across the room.

When she lifted the domes Amy almost clapped her hands with joy. There was a plate with bangers, sliced tomatoes, kippers, bacon and fried eggs. A silver toast holder held lightly toasted slices of bread. There was also a plate heaped with scones, bowls with clotted cream, strawberry jam, a small pot of soft creamy butter and a large silver tea pot, a magnificent full English breakfast.

"We thought you could do with a little bit of your old home."

Amy was touched that they had gone out of their way to make her first breakfast from the country she had lived in for so long.

"Thank you! I hope you will also thank Melita for her kindness. It's perfect!"

Glory smiled and left the room, closing the door behind her.

Amy was almost finished when there was a knock on the secret door. "Top of the mornin' to you. Did you have a good sleep? Are you ready to go?" Jimmy eyed the last uneaten piece of toast.

"Would you like it? I can't eat a bite more."

"Don't mind if I do." They both turned when Marie walked in and shut the door behind her.

"Jimmy, why am I not surprised? But this is early even for you. Listen, if she is to be the Pirate Queen I think you must take her to meet Michael today. There are many plans to be made."

"Exactly my thought." Jimmy tucked the toast into his vest pocket. "I will wait for you on the street."

Amy left her bedroom but not before watching Jimmy disappear. The secret door clicked shut behind him.

Remembering to take a jacket with her she went down the Grand Staircase, through the front door, passing the courtyard, under the Porte-Cochere and out to the street where Jimmy was leaning against the side of the building twirling a dark green bowler hat on one finger.

"We must make haste."

"Are we going to Leprechaun city below the street?"

"Later. Now we must hurry to catch Michael before he sails."

"Where is he going? And who is this Michael?"

Jimmy rushed along at a fast walk to keep up with Amy since he was not very tall.

"Michael is going to be the King at the Pirates Ball. This morning he's taking three families on his pirate ship The Golden Horn to Treasure Island."

"How exciting! Can we go, too?" This was more fun than she had even imagined it to be in all of her daydreams. Treasure Island!

"We'll see. It's an overnight scavenger hunt for buried treasure. I'm not sure about your being away overnight."

Amy clapped her hands. "Tell me all about Treasure Island. Where is it? Is there a big Pirate Hotel? And I want to hear all about this Pirates Ball."

"Actually you stay in caves that are so luxurious that.....we'll talk later...all in good time."

Amy passed three tour guides dressed as vampires. No wonder no one paid any attention to a Leprechaun in green velvet short pants and black and white checkered knee socks.

"Marie showed me Pirate's Alley yesterday. That's where I saw The Black Witch. Jimmy...she was in a carriage with horses and she...she... was flying in the air."

Jimmy looked at Amy and rolled his eyes. "The Black Witch is such a drama queen!"

Amy couldn't stop herself from giggling which led to all out laughing. Everyone they passed wondered what was so funny.

Jimmy led the way into The Sweet Shop on the corner of Pirate's Alley and Jackson Square. He waved a greeting to a woman selling candy behind a glass counter.

"That's Suzie, the owner." Jimmy waved to a small, pleasant looking woman wearing very thick glasses and sitting behind a glass candy case.

Suzie waved back and continued working on her crossword puzzle.

If it had been up to Amy she would have spent time wandering down the aisles filled with wonderful sweets of all sorts behind glass enclosed waist high cabinets.

Taking Amy's hand Jimmy headed for a door in the back of the shop marked Store Room. Suddenly Amy stopped causing Jimmy to stop.

"What's up?"

"I thought I saw someone I knew."

"How is that? You don't know anyone here."

"I thought it was the man who ran the ferry boat in Scotland. He brought Marie to the island."

"That's ridiculous. What would a Ferryman from Scotland be doing here? Sometimes we see someone who reminds us of someone we knew."

"I guess so." She was sure it was Seamus that she saw in the aisle with the giant pink lollipops. She couldn't think of even one reason for his being here. He must be following her. Why would he do that?

"Amy, my dear, after you." Jimmy held the door to the store room open.

They both stepped into a dimly lit room packed with brown boxes, labeled with various sweet treats, on one side of the wall. There was a door with an exit sign over it at the back leading to Pirate's Alley. And a huge brick wall with a sign saying HERE that pointed to an outline of a large hand.

Her eyes widened when Jimmy placed his hand against the wall in the directed spot and suddenly a solid wood door that wasn't there before was there now. Jimmy took his hand away and the door disappeared.

"Do the same."

Amy followed, putting her hand against the wall. The door reappeared and Jimmy went through, pulling her behind him.

"Jimmy, what did you do?"

"The hand can tell if you have any pirates in your family tree. If you do then a door opens and you get to go through. If you don't it's just a brick wall."

"This means I have a pirate in my family tree?"

"Oh my, yes. More than one. Very famous pirates indeed but I will tell you about it later."

The skies were overcast but everything else was different. The streets were filled with one fascinating shop after another. There were narrow alleyways between each building.

Families with young children in tow were rushing around talking about which pirate ride or which treasure shop they wanted to visit. No one paid any attention to them other to say excuse me, sorry, we're in such a rush, if you don't want to wait forever you have to get to the sunken galleon tour in Pirate Village right now.

"Where are we?"

"Pirate Village. Remember we entered by that secret door that allows someone to pass through only if they have a pirate in their family tree? That's where we are now."

"I heard someone say something about a park with rides."

"Over where the French Quarter ends at Esplanade Avenue is a park that has fabulous rides on pirate ships. You'll see lots of interesting gifts shops and cafes. There's even a Pirate Savings and Loan. By the way, Marie told you all about the Pirates Ball, right?"

"She mentioned a little about being the Pirate Queen but not about the ball. She said you would tell me everything."

Jimmy wiped his forehead with a handkerchief. "Just like her to pass it on to me but I guess she has a lot to deal with."

"You mean my Aunt Lily."

Jimmy rolled his eyes at her. "Another drama queen!"

"Yes, but one that doesn't fly." They both started laughing again.

"Small difference, believe me." Jimmy was laughing when he stepped in a puddle.

He sat on an concrete bench. Pulling off his socks he let the water pour out of his buckled shoes. "Don't worry about that, I dry quickly. Now about the Pirates Ball....it's a really big deal for the Pirates. Do you know anything about Mardi Gras?"

"I read about it in the Library at St. Luke's."

"Anyway, the Pirates have their own floats. The Krewe of Pirate World is...very old. You are to be the Pirate Queen and Michael will be the King at the Pirates Ball."

Amy sat next to him on the bench. "Jimmy,

Marie explained about the curse."

"That Marie, she beats me to everything. Very few people know about the curse. For all the pirates it will be a grand event to finally have a parade and a Queen for the Pirates Ball. And you, my dear Amy, will be a very special Queen."

"I have a feeling my Aunt would never have brought me back from the Orphanage except for the curse.

"You think?" Jimmy laughed. "Well, right you are."

"My mother's home is in the French Quarter. I know she's alive somewhere. I see her in my sleep sometimes. She calls out to me. She's lost. I...I—"

"I'm sorry about your Mom. I knew her. She was very kind."

"I think she wanted to be Pirate Queen. But she ran off with my Father instead. Maybe if I'm the Pirate Queen she will know and come back for me. What do I have to do as the Pirate Queen?"

"We have to go for your gown fitting later but first we have to get to the dock before Michael leaves." Jimmy took off at a fast little run and for once Amy had to hurry to keep up with him.

"I've seen, in books, all the fabulous gowns they wear at the Mardi Gras."

"Well, there you go! Maybe we'll stop at The Golden Lantern, a tavern on the waterfront patronized by all the pirates. Michael's dad, Charlie, owns the place. I've been there. The food is wonderful."

"This is all very exciting but I wish we had time to linger a bit. Do we get back to the French Quarter the same way we came in?"

"I think so." Jimmy looked at her like he wasn't sure. "Jimmy!"

"Of course we do." He smiled and patted her hand.

Amy followed Jimmy down streets lined with all varieties of shops and businesses. There was the Pirate Savings & Loan, Pirate Tours and Thrills, and tempting smells came from The Pirate Café.

She would have stopped in each one but Jimmy had her hand and was rushing her along. He promised they would return and visit every one.

"Jimmy, I read in the Library that many people came to Louisiana through Ellis Island in New York."

"I was one, my dear."

"How did you do that? I mean you're a Leprechaun. Someone must have noticed."

Jimmy laughed. "Well me older brother, Liam, went first and then sent for the rest of us. Actually it was easy. We barely have time but watch, I'll show you how we all got through the Port in New York. Stay here. And do not say a word!"

A family with six kids in tow and walking in almost single file down the sidewalk was headed in their direction. Jimmy walked towards them and then disappeared into a dark doorway. As they passed Amy heard the Dad say "Margie, don't we have six in our brood?"

"We do indeed, Edgar, why do you ask?"

"Well it seems we have seven now."

As the last child walked by, looking identical to the other six, he looked over at Amy and winked. He had the same blond hair, cropped short. He was wearing pants, a shirt and a vest in a dull grey cotton material that was far too big for him, just as his other siblings.

"Edgar, I do want to get to the Bayou Pirate ship ride so we'll sort it out later."

The number was reduced by one when they went past another doorway when the last child ducked in and came out looking once again like Jimmy O'Brien.

"Well that certainly is a trick."

"Nothing surprises you, Amy my girl."

"The first thing I saw when I got here was a woman all in black, driving four horses pulling a carriage and it was at least ten feet in the air. Today we went through a secret doorway to a place that I didn't know existed then you changed into...oh, never mind... and you think I'm going to be amazed by anything?" She had to remember to ask Jimmy just how he did that.

Amy caught a glimpse of someone walking with a slight limp. But he turned the corner and was out of sight before she had a chance to study him. He reminded her of Seamus, the Ferryboat man who brought mail and sometimes visitors to the orphanage. How silly, she thought. She was now starting to see Seamus everywhere.

Seamus had followed Amy and the little guy into the store room. He saw the HERE sign on the wall and placed his hand in the outline but nothing happened. Waste of time, he thought and rushed out the back door marked EXIT that led to Pirate's Alley. He expected to see them somewhere up or down the street but it was like they disappeared. He wandered up and down Pirate's Alley and the surrounding streets.

Turning, he saw a large garden enclosed with an elaborate and very high, black wrought iron fence. There was a statue of an old soldier sitting on a horse in the middle of the popular tourist location. A small brass sign said Jackson Square. Deciding they were somewhere in the tranquil tree lined square he raced over to begin his search anew.

The smell of something very sweet caught his attention so he headed across the street, to Café Du Monde. Everyone was eating sugar coated fried doughnuts and drinking mugs of coffee. Not one to pass up a sweet treat, and his belly attested to that fact, he figured he had time.

He tried to concentrate on what he was there for. He had never murdered anyone but he couldn't let Amy live now that her memory of that night was coming back. It was his family or her life. The fast moving waters of the Mississippi River would be a perfect place to dispose of a body. He'd eat first, think later. He couldn't do anything until he found her anyway.

Seamus sat down at a small, unoccupied table in the open air café and ordered.

He was eating his last doughnut when he felt something tugging at his pants leg. Looking under the table he exhaled in surprise, which is something you never do when you're eating fried doughnuts covered with powdered sugar.

A huge rat with a man's face and a rodent body was sitting up on his hind legs looking very distressed indeed. Powdered sugar drifted down around him making his whiskers twitch and he sneezed twice.

"Bon jour, Cher. Name's Bubba Boudreax. Not the best way to meet so next time keep the sugah to yourself!"

"I've never seen a French speaking rat before. Not one with a man's face."

"We're Cajuns from Bayou Lafourche. We speak Cajun French. There's a teeny difference...never you mind. Listen up, me and my River Rat brothers would also like to see the ...er...demise of Miss Amy. We noticed you've been watching her."

Seamus looked up to see if anyone was observing his strange behavior of talking to someone under the table.

Bubba's little rat paw tugged on Seamus's pants leg again. "You see we used to be plain old rats until the Black Witch...hey...you forget I say anything." Bubba looked around nervously like he expected the Black Witch to pop up any minute and smite him a fatal blow for just speaking her name.

Seamus definitely didn't want to draw attention to himself even though no one seemed to notice him at all.

"Just what is ye involvement in all this?" He whispered behind his napkin.

"Geez, you are big time nosy! We were a family of Cajun shrimpers when the Black Witch changed us into these...creatures. So...it's payback time."

"Why?"

"We have our reasons. It's need to know, Cher, and right now you don't need to know any more than that."

"Where can I find ye? Where do ye live?"

"River City. Got to go. We'll find you." Bubba twitched his whiskers and in a flash he disappeared.

A waiter, wiping his hands on a starched white apron, was instantly by his side. "Another order?"

"Yes, indeed. Best doughnuts I ever did have."

The waiter looked down his nose at Seamus, wrote on his pad, and quickly left. The very idea calling Beignets....doughnuts!

Jimmy hailed a carriage and told the driver to make haste getting them to Pirate Park.

Amy was thrilled to travel in one of the carriages Marie had told her about but she really wanted to stop along the way at The Pirate Gift Shop. A big sign proclaimed that the newest game in the storefront window was The Pirate Treasure Game with Pirate ships circling a detailed map and where it stopped you pillaged and plundered the town, gaining jewels in a treasure chest that could be exchanged for good things to eat and drink. But there was no time for that right now. Jimmy promised her that they would spend a day looking through all the stores and having something called fried alligator po'boys for lunch. She had read about alligators in books but the thought of eating one was not at all appetizing. Oh yuck!

The carriage stopped at the entrance sign to Pirate Park. Jimmy had a never ending supply of pieces of eight which everyone in this place seemed to use instead of cash.

"Jimmy, look!" Amy was fascinated with The Bayou Gold and Treasure Trip tour. And she also wanted to go on the glass enclosed pirate ship that went down the dunes, through mysterious caves and under the water to explore sunken chests filled with gold, silver and jewels.

She had never seen so many pirates before. Come to think of it outside of the many library books on pirates she had read she had never seen even one real pirate in her life and now they were all around her, all shapes, sizes and ages. And they looked very authentic, too.

They arrived at the dock just as the men were throwing off the lines, freeing the Pirate Ship, and readying it for departure to Treasure Island. They leaped onto the gangplank as it was starting to lift in the air and raced onto the boat.

"Cutting it close, Jimmy." A male voice boomed out behind Amy.

She turned and looked into blue eyes the color of the deepest part of the Irish Sea. Black hair fell over his forehead. He stood taller than her, at least six feet. He was dressed the part of an adventurous pirate with a billowing white shirt, and navy pantaloons. He was barefoot. If it was a costume it was a very authentic one. He had a red scarf tied around his neck and a weathered pirate three cornered hat on his head. Even if he was the most handsome man she'd ever met she wasn't going to let him talk to them that way.

"We got here as fast as we could. I didn't notice you holding the boat for us."

"Do they do that where you come from?"

"They most certainly do." "Amy, this is Michael McShane."

"Well then...they certainly do, Michael McShane!" Amy stressed his name in an uncharacteristically loud manner even for her.

"Did you have lunch yet?"

"Jimmy promised me a very tasty alligator...uh...French dip."

"That would be something to see. I imagine you mean po'boy." Michael laughed.

"What is a po'boy? And stop laughing at me."

Amy stormed away. She would much rather lean against the railing and watch the open water of the sea than stand there and be ridiculed.

Michael was occupied by the three families who had booked the Treasure Island tour. They each had lots of questions. He explained that they would be shipwrecked on a deserted island with a real pirate who would take them to their luxury cave accommodations and fix dinner for everyone. They would be visited by a band of more Pirates who would give them a treasure map. They had to work together to find the treasure chest filled with gold, silver and jewels. When they delivered it to the pirates they would be set free to return to the ship and sail back to the dock in Pirate Park.

Each family had several kids who were thrilled at the adventure.

Michael walked over and leaned against the railing next to Amy. She was certainly pretty if somewhat feisty.

"You are welcome to spend the night on the ship unless you'd like to stay in a cave and join in the treasure hunt."

"Stay overnight. I hope someone has told Marie where we are."

"The plans were that I was going to drop off my guests and take you back to the Park but that was before I got word that we're only slightly ahead of a huge storm headed our way so we're staying here for the night."

"Can Jimmy call Marie and tell her."

"I'm sure he's doing that right this minute."

"In that case if I am to stay then I would prefer a cave, thank you." Realizing that sounded really harsh she hastened to add. "I've never stayed in a cave before." Actually she'd never stayed anywhere but the orphanage but she didn't know him so she was certainly not going to talk to him about her personal life. And so far she didn't know whether she wanted to get to know him. He was rude from the first time they met. Not a good sign.

"It's really nice. Looks something like a hotel room. Big, comfortable bed. Air conditioning in the summer. I'll stay on the ship but if you need me Jimmy can send word."

"I'll be just fine, thank you." Amy crossed her arms and looked away.

Michael had things to do so he pushed away from the railing and walked off. Jimmy joined her looking down at the turbulent sea.

"You'll be getting your sea legs in no time."

"I love the sea. I grew up on an island. I could see the sea from just about any room in the orphanage."

Jimmy wanted to ask her about it but he didn't want to pry.

"Going to be a big storm very soon." "How do you know? Michael just told me." "Leprechaun weatherman on the TV just said so." "Really?"

Jimmy laughed. "See the dark clouds hanging low over the horizon?"

"Yes."

"That usually means wind, rain and a storm."

Amy laughed. "Jimmy, you always make me laugh."

"I do my best."

"Jimmy, did you call Marie and tell her we won't be home tonight?"

"I tried to call but I couldn't get through. She knows you're with me so she won't be worried."

Amy figured that made sense so she relaxed and started enjoying the ride.

"You said you'd tell me about the pirate in my family tree."

"Yes. Your great great great great grandfather. Oh...somebody in the family, married Marianne Teach, the only daughter of Edward Teach, who was known by the name of Blackbeard. The story goes that on one lovely spring day, after much contemplation, Edward sent Marianne to stay with a school friend and attend all the social parties of the season in New Orleans. To his horror,

Marianne fell in love with Governor Claiborne's son. They married when she was eighteen years old."

Although Amy wanted to pay attention to Jimmy's story, the pirate ship was approaching an island that caught her attention. The orphanage had been on a miserably cold island, with a rocky beach, right in the middle of the Irish Sea between Scotland and Ireland, nothing like this Island paradise with a glistening white sandy beach ringed by a fringe of palm trees.

Michael called for the gangplank to be lowered and everyone walked right onto the sandy beach.

A colorfully dressed pirate with a black patch over his left eye was leaning against a coconut tree.

Michael shook his hand and turned to speak to his guests. "This is One Eye. He will take you to your cave accommodations for the evening. One Eye and Jocko have a fantastic seafood BBQ planned for later. They will give you an itinerary for tomorrow's treasure chest hunt. If you need me for anything I'll be on my ship."

Turning to go back on board he waved to Amy and Jimmy.

Amy followed One Eye past the palm trees into a dense forest. Ferns, magnificent trees that bore flowers of all colors and sizes were home to multi colored parrots and other exotic birds that swooped through their thick branches. In some places it was so dense the sun barely touched the ground.

Amy dropped back to walk beside Jimmy for a while.

Still worried Amy said "I have to tell Marie I won't be back until tomorrow. Can I call from the room?"

"Oh, sure. The phone's right next to the TV."

"Jimmy! I take it they don't have phone service."

"Have you ever heard of a cave with a phone and TV?"

"I've never heard of a cave with a big bed and air conditioning!"

"Don't worry I took care of everything."

"What did you do?"

"Right after we got on board I sent a seagull with a message in its beak."

"I guess I wasn't paying

attention." "You think?"

Forgetting about the silliness of a seagull with a message in its beak, Amy sighed. "He is the most aggravating young man I've ever met."

"Met many?"

"No."

"There you are. All young men his age are a bit aggravating. But they grow out of it."

They arrived at the first of the cave accommodations. The sun was starting to set and a threat of heavy rain was in the air.

Amy and Jimmy were the last to get their keys.

Amy was eager to see her room but she had to wait while One Eye explained that they were all going to meet on the beach for a bonfire and the promised seafood BBQ in one hour, weather permitting.

The weather held out even though you could hear thunder and see the lightning in the distance.

One Eye and Jocko sure could cook. It was a seafood feast with lobster, shrimp and a variety of things from the sea in a big bowl. Hunks of French bread were for mopping up the juices. And there was a big barrel of home churned chocolate ice cream for dessert. Everyone ate with great delight.

Before they were finished, and much to the glee of the children, three more pirates strolled down the beach and stopped at their bonfire. They handed out treasure maps and made sure everyone understood all the directions for finding the pirate treasure chests. They sang a few charming pirate songs and then disappeared into the jungle beyond the sandy beach.

With their children beyond excited parents rounded up their families and headed back to their caves in hopes of a good night's sleep before the early morning adventure.

Her room was right next to Jimmy's. She was delighted to see that someone had lit her fireplace, which made it very cozy. A plush robe with a floor length flannel nightgown were draped over the bed. Firelight bounced off the walls. She was soon fast asleep in a most extraordinary bed built right into the stone wall of the cave. Soft down comforters over and under her felt like she was sleeping on a cloud.

A storm roared outside but she felt safe and happy.

Someone was calling her name. She knew the voice. "Be my brave little girl." It was the last thing she remembered her mother saying to her when they lowered her into the raging sea in the lifeboat. ".....my brave little girl."

"Mama!" Amy woke up crying and choking at the same time. The winds had turned and smoke from the fireplace was filling the room.

Amy, Queen of the Pirates Ball

CHAPTER FOUR
Seamus Stalks Amy/Cajun Rats Get Involved

Amy grabbed a robe, threw open her door and raced out into the middle of the storm. Ferns, bent almost in half to the ground, whipped back and forth in a frenzy. Small animals darted around frantic to find shelter. Anything lighter was airborne in seconds.

She pounded on Jimmy's door but no one answered. The door was unlocked but Jimmy was not inside. There was even more smoke in his room.

Her next thought was to seek shelter in the huge ship. Turning, she raced down to the beach. The waiting ship had its gangplank down and ready to bring anyone aboard who sought refuge.

As she struggled against the wind she staggered.

Suddenly she was swept off her feet, lifted by strong male arms, and carried the rest of the way aboard.

It would have been wonderful if her hero hadn't been complaining nonstop.

"That was the stupidest thing anyone has done. If you had been blown off the ramp you could have drowned. Why did you leave your room in this storm?" Michael demanded.

"It wasn't a room as much as it was a cave." Amy could feel her chin start to tremble.

"You can put me down now. I can walk, you know..."

"Right." Michael opened the door to the Captain's Quarters, walked inside, and carefully placed her on a small sofa.

"...and all the smoke from the fireplace came down the chimney and I was sure I heard my Mother calling for me and..."

Amy did something she rarely did, let alone in front of a stranger, she started crying. Everything was just too much for her. She had left the Orphanage, the only home she'd ever known, and moved to a house where her aunt was barely civil to her. She had moved to a place where a Black Witch drove a horse drawn carriage high in the air above the street and her best, and only friend, in this strange place was a magical Leprechaun who could make not only himself disappear and come back but he could make secret doors appear leading to places she didn't even know existed. And now she couldn't find him.

Michael just sat next to her and held her hand.

After a while Amy looked around. Burgundy velvet drapes hung at the large windows. Glossy wood furniture filled the small room. There was a Captain's desk with all manner of small and large drawers for papers, nautical maps and things. A lovely heavy wood bed built into the wall was hidden by its own brocade hangings with tie backs.

"This is a lovely room. Thank you." Amy braced herself against the bed railing. The storm made the ship rock in a not very gentle way.

"Nature fights back."

Amy started laughing which made crying very hard to do at the same time.

Michael laughed along with her.

"Is anybody else here?"

"Just you and the family with the twin boys. They said their chimney had a problem, too. Would you like a cup of tea?"

"I would. Thank you."

Michael went to a panel in the wall and pushed a button. The wall slid open to reveal a small but very compact kitchen.

"I heard my Mom calling me. I know I heard her. But it was all confused. Like she was far away. And someone is following me. Jimmy told me it was probably someone who looked like someone I know but that's not true."

He placed a tray with a teapot, a jug of cream and a bowl of sugar on the table in front of the sofa.

"Who is this person following you?"

"His name is Seamus; he's the ferryman in Ireland who took us from the island to the mainland where we caught the train."

Amy poured a little cream in her cup.

"Where did you see him?"

"In the Sweet Shop by Jackson Square. I know it was him."

"And it wasn't someone who maybe looked liked that guy?"

"What is this? First Jimmy and now you. I know what I saw."

"Okay. Drink your tea. It will help. And if you see him again tell me right away, okay?"

Michael leaned back in his seat. "Why don't you tell me a little about your life before you got here."

"Until a few days ago I was living at St. Luke's Orphanage off the coast of Scotland in the Irish Sea. I remember being on a big boat with my Mom. I was very young. Five years old...I know because it was my birthday. Very loud alarms went off. They put me in a small boat with many children. That was the last time I saw my Mom, almost thirteen years ago.

The next memory I have is someone putting me on top of an overturned lifeboat. And then we were picked up from the water by a fisherman...the same man that's following me now.

When he took me to the mainland Marie thanked him for saving me. It was then I remembered there was someone else in the water with me. The man who helped me get on top the boat. When I said so, Seamus, the ferryman, said it was not true. He said I was alone. But I remember they knew each other very well because he hugged the man and was crying he was so happy."

"And then this fisherman, Seamus, became the ferryboat man?"

Amy nodded. "I talked to Seamus now and then when Mrs. Johnston sent me to meet the boat with something for him to mail on the mainland."

"I see." Michael kept to himself the fact that as Ferryman he could keep an eye on Amy. He could be following her right now and Michael didn't think it was for anything good.

"We have guest cabins aboard. I'll get word to Jimmy that you're here."

"That would be very nice only I can't find Jimmy. He wasn't in his room."

"I have an idea where he is. Every now and then he comes on the Treasure Hunt and spends the night fleecing the pirates out of their pieces of eight. Jimmy is a terrific poker player."

At that moment the door to the Captain's Quarters burst open and Jimmy raced inside.

"Amy, thank goodness, I have been looking all over for you."

Amy looked at Michael who was trying his best to keep from laughing.

"The question is...where have you been, Jimmy?" Amy noticed that his vest pockets were bulging.

Jimmy decided to sit on a footstool before he toppled over with the weight of his burden. "I couldn't sleep so I went over to have a chat with the Pirates." He pulled the stool close to the sofa where Amy was sitting so he could get into this story he was hoping she'd believe. "Then this horrible storm came up and I was stuck there. Then the storm abated..." He realized the stool had somehow turned and he was now talking to the wall so he turned back to Amy. As he swung around on the stool a coin fell out of his pocket. He didn't notice it since he kept talking. "And when I got back you were gone and your room was full of smoke."

"Why are your pockets filled with gold coins? Jimmy, did you spend the night playing cards with the pirates?"

Jimmy looked down snatching up the coin. He smacked his knee and laughed. "Sure and I did, Darlin', ya have a keen nose, ya do."

"Here I was worried to death about you and you were out partying!"

Jimmy almost fell off the footstool laughing and then just as he was starting to wave a finger in the air to make a point he passed out from total exhaustion.

"Well, somebody had a really good time." Michael picked him up while Amy opened the door and followed Michael down the hall to a guest suite.

She waited outside while Michael left Jimmy on top of the bed with a coverlet over him and a pillow under his head.

When Michael returned he found Amy sitting on the floor fast asleep. He put her in a guest suite next to Jimmy.

Michael went back to his quarters. Tomorrow was going to be a very busy day.

Amy awoke to find someone had retrieved her clothes and they were cleaned, pressed and folded over a chair a few feet from where she had been sleeping.

Realizing she'd overslept she quickly showered and dressed.

Going topside she found all the families sprinting into the forest beyond the beach. They all had their treasure maps in hand.

Jimmy had a map of his own that he was examining intently.

He waved her over.

"Jimmy, I'm up for a good breakfast. How about you?"

He handed her a sandwich wrapped in wax paper and a bottle of orange juice. "Here you go. Breakfast of champions. Don't complain. You're late." He went back to the map.

Amy sighed. "I wasn't going to complain. And I happen to love ice cold egg sandwiches!"

Jimmy looked over the top of his reading glasses. "Now that I just don't believe."

They both started laughing.

"Look here, Amy. Everyone has their first clue and they're already off on the treasure hunt. Lucky for us I know this island very well. This is our first clue... Into a cave and over a fall

Brings you to the biggest tree of all.

Don't be surprised if its shape is round

But what a hoot it's growing upside down!

"I know where there's a cave that opens to a waterfall. Let's go!"

Jimmy led the way through the thickest part of the forest. She wondered if the treasure would be jewels or pieces of eight.

They came to an abrupt stop right in front of a huge flat stone. Jimmy disappeared behind a tree and a narrow door in the stone barely slid open allowing them to squeeze inside.

"Wow. Do you have a flashlight?"

"Don't need one. See the light at the end? That's the waterfall." Jimmy rushed inside. "Hurry up, Amy. We don't have all day."

"Good grief! You've certainly turned bossy."

Jimmy led the way through the cave grumbling all the while.

"I didn't get enough sleep."

"And whose fault was <u>that</u>?"

When they finally stepped out into the sunlight a huge waterfall thundered in front of them. Looking down made Amy dizzy.

Jimmy took the well traveled footpath to the top.

Amy, scrambling to stay with him, was relieved they didn't have far to go.

Sure enough, a tree blown over by a storm was growing upside down over a small pond of calm water. A red bandana was tied at the end of the longest branch with a paper attached to it. Anyone brave enough to climb out on the tree limb might easily fall into the little pond.

Amy sat down and unwrapped her sandwich. "Obviously I have to eat my breakfast so I guess you're elected to get that little piece of paper dangling out there."

Jimmy straddled the huge tree and grumbled all the way out to the bandana.

"I can hear you."

"I guess your hunger didn't interfere with your hearing."

"Nope. So what does it say?"
"Look to your left whilst hanging upside down
and you'll see a lovely sight called Pirate Town.
Stop at the Blue Goose Inn and say hello. We'll
give you your final clue before you go."

Jimmy, hanging upside down, started laughing. "We're going to pay a visit to me ole friends, me dear."

"I'm ready to go." She really didn't find a cold egg sandwich very appetizing so she left it behind for the little animals to find.

Jimmy led the way towards the pirates' hangout, The Blue Goose Inn.

Amy loved this Treasure Island Adventure. The Blue Goose Inn looked like it was right out of a Colonial village like Williamsburg, Virginia in America. A small sign hung on two rusty chains over the door creaked in the wind. There were posts for tying up horses. She closed her eyes and could almost hear the sound of the horse's hooves on the cobblestones under her feet. Amy couldn't leave the orphanage but she didn't need to since the library had a large section filled with travel books.

From the minute they walked through the doors the pirates had a million questions for Amy. She recognized One Eye and Jocko from the barbeque on the beach.

"Amy, this is Redbeard, Peter and Jean Claude." The pirates were instantly on their feet introducing themselves. They were thrilled she was going to be the Pirate Queen having missed having a parade and a ball for many years.

Redbeard and Peter offered her a fried chicken leg and some potato salad saying it was Fourth of July picnic food that she had missed all those years living on that cold rocky island in a far off land. Jean Claude brought her a glass of sweet ice tea. She was surprised they knew so much about her.

The Blue Goose Inn had a tavern downstairs and overnight accommodations on the second floor. Amy wondered if smoke filled cave rooms kept them busy.

The Pirates were charming and explained that any spare time outside of being Inn keepers was spent making items for the gift shop in Pirate Village. Every time Michael brought a group over for the Treasure Hunt they made sure he returned with a box of items to be delivered and sold at the Pirate Gift shop.

Amy teased the pirates saying she would not find the treasure unless they gave her the last clue. The friendly pirates told her that no one would get this treasure because it was given just to her but she would have to be patient and stay a little longer since they were enjoying her company so much.

Finally their stay was at an end. They reluctantly said goodbye to Amy and handed Jimmy the last clue, but not before reminding him that this treasure was for Amy to keep for her own.

Go to the beach on the other side

Be sure and get there before high tide.

Behind a big rock you're find an untidy heap

Dig a foot deep and what you find, you keep!

"See you next time around, guys!"

"We hope it's not anytime soon or we'll have to hide all our pieces of gold." The pirates laughed. "Tell Michael we're sending Big Joe over with our usual crafts for the gift shop."

"Will do!"

Jimmy took off so fast Amy had to hurry to keep up with him.

"What crafts do they make, Jimmy?"

"For one they make the boards for The Pirate Treasure Game Games. And also ships inside glass bottles—"

"—and treasure maps inside the bottles, too?"

Jimmy laughed. "Yes, those too. The Pirate Treasure Game has treasure maps inside glass bottles but those are very old."

"How exciting. I can't wait to play that game."

"All in good time. There are so many things to do first." "Like find our own treasure?"

"Exactly. And we have to get there before high tide. The treasure is buried in the sand."

"Oh, this is exciting."

They rushed through a dense tropical forest. There were mangoes, grapefruit, pears, apples and some fruits she didn't even have a name for, but had seen in books.

The sun was slanting on the sandy beach, which meant it was getting late. Jimmy knew Michael wouldn't leave without them but he was going to be really mad for throwing him off his schedule.

There was only one massive boulder on the small beach. They quickly dug through the pile of kelp. One foot down they found a small treasure chest. Inside was a beautiful apple green jade heart on a chain with a note asking if Amy would wear the jade heart at the Pirates Ball. There were also some gold coins for Jimmy which made him very happy.

Amy slipped the chain with the apple green jade heart around her neck. She felt a tingle from the heart as it lay warm against her throat. She didn't have time to think about that since Jimmy was urging them to hurry back to the ship.

When they got back Amy could see Michael pacing up and down on the main deck.

Jimmy sprinted up the gangplank. Michael began a heated debate with him while she struggled up the walkway. She decided right then that she would join one of those gym places some of the guests on the boat had been talking about. She needed to get in better shape if she was going to keep up with Jimmy.

Michael was busy from the moment she got on deck so there was little time to talk to him. She wasn't sure he was of a mind to talk to her anyway. Throwing him off his schedule had put him in a very bad mood.

It certainly didn't bother Jimmy too much since he was all smiles when he found her standing at the railing looking out at the sea.

"Be ready early tomorrow morning and we'll go for the dress fitting for your Queen's gown then we'll have Breakfast at Brennan's."

"What is Brennan's?"

"A famous restaurant in the French Quarter."

"Wonderful!"

It was almost dark when they finally docked.

Jimmy rushed them off the ship to a waiting carriage. She thought Michael was very handsome and had hoped to make amends over her behavior that afternoon but Jimmy didn't give her time to stay and chat other than a quick thank you.

"We have to hurry or we'll get caught in the parade."

"What does that mean?"

"You'll see."

"Are you sure Aunt Lily is not angry with me for being away overnight?"

"I am positive." The person Jimmy was worried about was Marie. She was probably pacing the floor right now. But at least telling her they were going to the dress fitting for the Queen's gown tomorrow morning was doing one more thing on Marie's to-do list. That should make her happy.

"Jimmy, you didn't tell me what time we're going to meet in the morning."

"I'll wait for you in front at eight o'clock. And don't eat breakfast. I will tell Marie we're going for your gown fitting and out for breakfast and then we'll explore the shops in Pirate Village. It's going to be a long day."

"I'm exhausted already."

"Amy, we've only just begun. We have so much to do."

The carriage dropped them off in a deserted alleyway in front of a brick wall with an outline of a hand. They placed their hands in the space marked and a door appeared. They went through ending up in the storeroom of an antique store on Toulouse Street.

It was pandemonium on the streets in the French Quarter. Police officers on horseback and on foot were kept busy keeping the swelling number of people back behind wood barricades.

"Where's The Sweet Shop?"

"There are a number of different entrance and exit points. We can go and come at our convenience which is not always the same place. Oh, you'll see, you'll see."

Amy had to walk fast to keep up with him.

Seamus was waiting in Jackson Square where he had a great view of the front entrance to the Sweet Shop. He figured if she went in that way then eventually she'd come out that way. He checked his watch. It was getting very late. Crowds of Mardi Gras revelers blocked his view.

Bubba, his new River Rat friend, climbed up on the concrete bench and sat next to him.

"You still here, Cher?"

"They went in yesterday morning and haven't come out yet."

"Ooooh. You been here all that time? You shoulda asked me. They went on a little boat trip."

"How do ye know that?"

"The nose knows!"

"Oh, good grief! Speak English, or at least your version of it, please."

"Not nice to make fun of Cajuns. Especially ones you need to help you."

Seamus gritted his teeth. How in the world did he get dependent on this group of rat people? But he did need their help so he plastered a smile on his face. "I am truly sorry. Staying up all night has made me a bit out of sorts."

"Whew! I'll say. Now I know where they are, I know when they're gittin' back and I know where they're goin' when they git back. They goin' to her house right now."

"And ye know that because...?"

"My brother Bobby was a stowaway on that ship they were on. He told me right away when they docked."

"We're partners, yes. So why don't ye just tell me what ye know."

"We'll meet here tomorrow morning early...like eight AM. They gotta pass by since the restaurant, where they have reservations in the morning, is just a little ways down the street."

"I want to follow them when they go into that sweet shop. I want to see where they go."

"Nope. You can't go there."

"Where do they go that I can't go?"

"Need to know, cher. And—" "—

Yeah. I've heard it before."

"You know you catch on fast, cher, for someone who is not Cajun!" Bubba's little rat body jiggled with glee.

Seamus was beginning to really dislike the little rat. Right now he needed his help but once Amy was out of the way Seamus had plans to do away with Bubba and his irritating high pitched squeal of a voice. Seamus looked down at Bubba and smiled. He hoped the scrawny little rat couldn't read his mind. That would not do at all, not at all. But Bubba seemed oblivious to everything but his successful plans for the following day.

"Where are they going tomorrow? Ye said something about a restaurant."

"It's right down there a ways. They have a reservation. That's when we strike."

Bubba reached up and put his little rat paw on his arm. "Too many tourists right now. See ya tomorrow."

Amy and Jimmy came out of the back door of the storeroom into the street right in the middle of a crowd of tourists moving this way and that.

"What's going on?" Amy was shoved aside almost losing sight of Jimmy.

"It's less than two weeks before Mardi Gras day. There are parades with floats every night and tons of tourists in the French Quarter all day and long into the night."

"Can we stand here and watch?" Jimmy

gave her a frustrated look. "No." "Can

we see a parade tomorrow night?"

"Maybe. But right now this will not do at all. It will take forever to get to your house."

We're going to take a bit of a shortcut. Stay close behind me."

Jimmy ducked into the lobby of The Golden Palace, a small, but opulent hotel.

"This hotel was built by Jean Lafitte in the early 1800s."

Amy wanted to stay and look around but Jimmy rushed her through to the courtyard in the rear. It was a beautiful flower filled space, with a splashing fountain, cobblestone courtyard and bordered by a thick grove of bamboo with ferns and palm trees in lush, tropical abundance.

Gas lanterns, on rusted poles, illuminated the pathways.

Looking around to make sure there was no one around he parted a spot in the bamboo and unlocked a small door.

"Keep up."

Amy followed Jimmy into a tiny space with steps leading down and down. She felt a little like Alice in Wonderland.

Pulling out a small flashlight Jimmy made his way down dark staircase that finally leveled into a tunnel. "Jean Lafitte was seeing Serena who worked as a kitchen maid in your home. He built this tunnel for two reasons. He smuggled European goods from his pirate ship into the hotel to sell tax free in the Americas. And he used this tunnel to sneak Serena out of the house and bring her to his hotel."

"Jimmy, that is so romantic. What happened to Serena and Jean Lafitte?"

"When the Claiborne family found out about her nightly trysts Serena lost her job at the big house."

"That wasn't very nice."

"The Claiborne's and Lafitte were not exactly friends. Then Serena disappeared."

"That's so sad. Did they ever get together?"

"No one knows. Lafitte left the running of his hotel to one of his pirate friends and sailed his ship into Caribbean waters. It is said he became very wealthy raiding ships that carried gold and silver to Spain and France. It was rumored that Serena had a son by Lafitte."

"Oh, Jimmy. Do you think if she had a son that he might still be alive?"

"Maybe."

Jimmy didn't want to get into dates and years. Serena was born about 1790. She returned to the French Quarter with the power to give herself and her son immortality. Today she is about two hundred and twenty years old and if she had a son he would be two hundred years old. What he didn't want to tell Amy was that Serena came back to the French Quarter and was now known to just a few as the Black Witch. A two hundred and twenty year old Black Witch! He wasn't sure how Amy would take that information. And he definitely didn't want to tell Amy that he was hundreds of years old, as were all his brothers. He would tell her all in good time. Slowly.

It seemed like they had walked forever when Jimmy stopped short.

"Are we here?"

"Almost, but first I want to show you something. Stand behind me and watch."

He pressed a stone in the wall of the tunnel. It looked like just one of the hundreds of other stones that were embedded in the walls.

A hole in the tunnel floor opened about ten feet down the passageway.

"Watch where you step. You do not want to fall into that."

They both peered over the edge into a black void.

"Did Jean Lafitte dig this pit?"

"Yes. When he was pursued by the law he would lead them into the tunnel and just when they thought they had him he would push the stone and they'd fall into the hole. By the time they got out he was gone."

"How incredible."

"Lafitte would escape through a secret door into the Claiborne house."

"Wouldn't someone in the house see him?"

"At the time your bedroom was used as a storeroom. It was a terrific hiding place and also a place for meeting Serena."

"That was very clever."

"Lafitte was a very clever man." Jimmy pushed the stone again and the hole silently closed over.

"Where does this go?"

"Leprechaun City. I will take you there but not now. I have to get you home right now."

They continued on a bit before Jimmy stopped and pushed a round stone in the wall. A door sprung open. Much to Amy's surprise the doorway led right into her bedroom. It was the door beside the fireplace.

What was not a surprise to Jimmy was the sight of Marie sitting in the wing chair by the fireplace with a very angry look on her face. Jimmy stopped short which caused Amy to almost run into him. "Now, Marie, just give it a second. We have a fitting scheduled for tomorrow morning. And then we'll go see about the throws. We spent the last two days with Michael on his ship. Once it was under sail we couldn't get off and—"

"---Be quiet! Do you know how much worry you've caused me? Why didn't you pick up a phone and call?"

"Well, me dear, you know there are no phones on Treasure Island."

Marie put the back of her hand to her forehead like a damsel in distress. "You took Amy to Treasure Island? Are you crazy?"

"It was ever so wonderful, Marie." Amy's enthusiasm waned when Marie turned to her with a look of supreme displeasure.

"Don't go that far away again."

"Okay. I do promise. But I had such a good time."

Marie wasn't finished with Jimmy who was now partly hiding behind the drapes that surrounded the bed.

"And you do this again and I promise I'll personally see you back to your tree house in Ireland. Understand?"

"Yes." Jimmy's voice wavered. "Well, I'll not dally. See you in the morning, Amy." In two seconds Jimmy was through the secret door. Amy heard it lock behind him.

"I hope I didn't worry Aunt Lily."

Marie sighed in frustration. "Don't mention this to her."

"Look what the pirates on Treasure Island gave me." Amy showed off the jade heart.

Marie was silent for what seemed forever. "That heart belonged to your Mother. It was her most cherished possession. She was wearing it when she left home."

"Then I will cherish it." Amy held it in her hand.

"Jimmy!" Marie looked directly at him in a very stern manner. "Please ask the pirates where they got the heart. Okay?"

Marie left Amy's bedroom wondering if that jade heart would be just the thing to bring Celeste back to them.

Amy wondered where the pirates got it.

She held the warm jade heart in the palm of her hand. When she closed her fingers around it she could feel a slight tingle. She concentrated on her Mother's voice.

"Madame Celeste? Madame Celeste?" The young girl touched her teacher's hand. Her teacher seemed far away in her thoughts.

"Oh, sorry, day dreaming as usual." Celeste smiled. "What is it Christina?"

"The bell. You told me to remind you about the bell not working."

"Yes, thank you. I will call the children inside myself."

Celeste stood in the doorway of the schoolhouse and watched the children playing on the swings. The building was comprised of six classrooms, a dining room, a library and a large meeting room. It had been the Town Hall in the 1800s. Her third and fourth grade classes were the last ones to leave the playground. The other teachers had already started their classes. The voice of children and teachers could be heard in a loud jumble from open windows with delicate lace curtains blowing the sounds in and out with the breeze.

Beckoning for the children to come inside she counted heads as they filed past her. Christina was her favorite. She reminded her so much of someone she just couldn't quite remember. Someone with the same long, silky black hair, fair skin and dark eyes so much like her own. Many of the French families had married Spanish fisherman.

Her life had started thirteen years ago when she woke up on a beach near the harbor of this same village. No one knew how she got there and no one could tell her anything about who she was, where she came from, or who found her.

The nuns at the school told her there had been a hand written note in her pocket. The unknown fisherman who found her said, in the note, that she was with someone he assumed was her husband since she was wearing a gold wedding band. The fisherman heard a man call out to her saying "Je t'aime, Celeste. Je t'aime." The fisherman pulled

Celeste into the boat but when he tried to help the man he had disappeared in the turbulent water.

The nuns reported that she spoke fluent French and English, and had a wonderful way with children, so the town fathers decided she would teach at the school. They knew that, one day, her memory would come back she would leave to return to a home that missed her.

The next morning Jimmy was waiting for Amy in front of the house. Amy hurried alongside Jimmy who seemed in a terrible rush.

"Could we just slow down for a bit?"

"No, we can't. The seamstress is expecting us and then we have reservations for brunch."

"Ah, yes, the famous Brennan's."

"Yes, so do walk faster."

"You have become the grumpiest person lately."

"And I will be until we get all the things done for the Pirates Ball."

The streets of the French Quarter went by in a whirl until they finally stood in front of a narrow house aptly called a shotgun cottage since if you stood in the front door and shot off a shotgun the bullet would go straight through to the back porch without touching one wall.

The cottage was painted with Caribbean pastel colors of turquoise, salmon colored shutters, off white trim and an ornate black wrought iron fence surrounded the house. A young girl, dressed in a long cotton skirt of colorful colors and a red bandana wrapped around her head stood in the doorway smiling at them.

"Amy, that's LouLou. She makes all the Queen gowns for the big Balls. Last year she took on making all the costumes for Babylon. They put on *Around the World in Eighty Days.* So she designed not only all the costumes for the play, the King and Queen costumes and all the costumes for the crew riding on the floats. It was quite something fabulous to see.

"How ya doin' dawlin'? Ya'll come on in." LouLou beckoned them inside.

"Thank you for seeing us on such short notice." Amy smiled at LouLou who nodded in return. "Jimmy was just telling me about your wonderful designs. Last year you did the costumes for Babylon."

"Thank ya! I haven't made anything for the Pirates Ball in ages so this is exciting for me." As Amy passed by her she heard LouLou say to Jimmy "Oh, my Gawd, she is sure gonna make a pretty Pirate Queen."

Amy blushed but a second later her attention was diverted by the rich fabrics scattered here and there on gleaming mahogany dining tables piled high with silks, satins, silk velvet in every color imaginable and bolts of delicate gold and silver cloth. There were giant reels of silver thread side by side with threads of all the colors of a child's crayon box. And there were boxes of white ermine in long strips hanging from slightly open lids. There were tables of tulle dusted with glittering colors.

It didn't take the young girl long to whip out a measuring tape while at the same time pinning a paper form around Amy's slim body pinning and drawing a most intricate pattern. She also used a thick pen to make notations on a pad.

Amy's eyes widened when she saw gold silk and silver lame material and a large reel of gold silk thread on a separate table.

"LouLou, is that the material for my gown?"

"Yes. Only the best."

"It's so beautiful. It's going to be a gown out of a fairy tale."

"Amy, me dear, 'tis indeed since it's a gown fit for the Pirate Queen." Jimmy smiled.

LouLou finished quickly. Opening the front door she waved Jimmy and Amy off into the street. "Ya'll come back in three days. Take care now, dawlin'."

Although hurrying to keep up with Jimmy, Amy turned and waved back. "Where is LouLou from? I mean her accent?"

"Metairie."

"I see." She certainly didn't see but there were so many strange things about this wonderful city. She wanted to ask Jimmy about Metairie but she was sure she'd get the hang of things after a while.

"Now we are off for that fantastic feast I promised you."

Luckily an empty French Quarter carriage was passing by so Amy and Jimmy hopped inside and away they went. Jimmy ordered the carriage to stop at the Sweet Shop.

"We can walk from here."

Jimmy was thrilled they were getting all the Queen chores out of the way. "We only have one thing left to do. We have to get your throws. The stuff you throw to the crowds."

"Well, I sure hope we do it in a slower manner than this morning. I'm going to be exhausted before this ball begins."

"We'll get the throws later. First we have a reservation and I'm trying to get us there in time."

"Oh."

Amy kept quiet after that. She certainly didn't want to miss this well talked about breakfast.

They passed a most beautiful church that Jimmy told her was called the Saint Louis Cathedral, and hurried on.

Seamus sat patiently waiting on a bench in the Park. Bubba climbed up beside him. Minutes later they watched Amy and the little guy coming down the street and they weren't walking slowly.

Bubba jiggled with glee. "I told ya. I told ya. They're on their way to the restaurant."

They watched Amy and Jimmy hurry on their way.

Seamus pushed off the park bench and stayed behind them moving unseen from one doorway to another.

Bubba climbed up his pants leg and onto his shoulder.

"Slow down. I have it all taken care of. My brother Tommy's got it all under control, cher. Just you see."

"What does he plan on doing?"

"He hangs out at the restaurants. Knows his way around. He's gonna put a little surprise in her food before it leaves the kitchen."

"He's got to knock her off. He knows, right?"

"Trust me. It's not his first. Know what I mean?"

"I have to stay out of sight. She might recognize me."

"Wait in the Park. But first drop me off in the alley behind the restaurant."

Amy and Jimmy put their names on the long list and waited patiently to be called. When Amy finally heard her name called they went to the front of the line.

"Table six, outside." Someone shouted out to a waiter who indicated that they should follow him to an outdoor patio and a table under a huge moss draped oak tree.

A very dapper River Rat was watching, waiting to hear the table number. He passed the information on.

Jimmy ordered for them. "We'll both have Eggs Benedict and Banana Foster. Thank you."

"Isn't Banana Foster a dessert?"

Jimmy smiled. "Yes. A most famous dessert at Brennan's. And why not. You're so thin a good strong wind could blow you away."

Amy laughed.

"You know there's a saying...life is uncertain, eat dessert first!"

"You are a scoundrel, Jimmy O'Brien!"

"Whew, is that all. I've been called worse."

Closing the menus he handed them back to their waiter who quietly left with their order on its way.

"I haven't been here in a long time." Jimmy brushed a leaf off the table.

A River Rat hiding under their table rushed off.
"Jimmy, it's lovely here."

The old red bricks in a herringbone pattern underfoot looked like they had been there for a hundred years. Wind whistled through the oak trees making the moss sway back and forth in the breeze. It was perfect weather for eating outside.

The Black Witch roamed around her spacious French Quarter mansion. Something was brewing. Someone close to her was in danger.

She found herself beside a pond in the center of her courtyard. It had been ages since she'd studied the waters. She gazed deeply into the depths and demanded to see the past, present, and what lay ahead.

The waters stilled. She saw her beloved son, Philippe, holding an infant wrapped in a pink silk blanket in his arms. She heard his voice. "Our beautiful daughter, Amelia."

A woman appeared next to him. It was Celeste Claiborne.

"Amelia....sounds so formal, Philippe. I want to call her Amy."

"Amy, it is."

Serena knew that Amy was the name of the young girl with Marie being driven to the Claiborne home. The young girl had powers far more than she knew. Serena was invisible to all but blood relations. Amy saw her flying through the air. Not many could do that. Serena knew at that instant that the young girl with Marie was her granddaughter, Philippe's child.

The Black Witch waved her arms in the air. Thunderclouds gathered overhead. Lightening crashed all around her. Amy was in danger. She had to act quickly.

Speaking in a low rhythmic tone she cast a Protection Spell around Amy.

"Protect her now and keep her safe.

Let no hand cause her harm,
Or they will wish they had not been born."

In no time they were finished and while they were waiting for the Bananas Foster Amy and Jimmy laughed about the silliest of things.

Suddenly Amy felt like something stabbed her in the stomach. She was so sick she couldn't stay in her seat. Her legs started cramping and all she wanted to do was get up and walk. Certainly as far away from the restaurant as possible. She had never felt like this before. "I feel terrible."

It wasn't the Eggs Benedict because he ate the same thing and he was fine.

At that moment their waiter came to take away the dishes and Jimmy thrust a One Hundred Dollar bill in his hand.

"This is to pay for the entire meal. We have to go. Something has come up."

"But the Bananas Foster desserts are on the way. Look, see they're flaming them right this minute."

Jimmy grabbed Amy's hand and they exited quickly.

Just as fast, a young honeymoon couple took their table.

"What is that?" The young man inquired as the flaming banana dessert was being rolled up to their table.

"A very famous Brennan dish called Bananas Foster." The waiter didn't know what to do. This had never happened before. Never at Brennan's.

"Oh, John, let's have that. I've heard of it. It's supposed to be divine."

"Actually, it's paid for. You're welcome to it right now, if you like."

The young bride clapped her hands. "I'd love it."

"If it's already paid for we can't let it going to waste, can we?" The young man was thinking of his appetite.

They watched the waiter pour more rum over the sautéed brown sugar, butter and sliced bananas. Then he set it afire again. It was very dramatic. And served with a scoop of homemade vanilla ice cream.

The young couple couldn't wait to dig into this sweet treat. It was only a few minutes later when they both keeled over and fell from their chairs right onto the red brick patio floor.

Amy, Queen of the Pirates Ball

CHAPTER FIVE

A Haunted Plantation

There was a mass panic in the restaurant.

Luckily a Doctor was seated just a few tables away and he was at their side immediately. The Doctor smelled the dish that had once held the dessert.

He looked up at the restaurant manager who had rushed over and was trembling in fear.

"Someone put old fashioned knock out drops in their dessert. But not to worry. They will recover. Could someone call for an ambulance?"

Bubba was standing on his little rat feet peering out from behind the Queen Fern in the corner of the restaurant. Tommy scurried up right beside him.

"Hey, cher. I knock em out like you say. Dem people topple over like trees in da wind." He giggled with glee.

Bubba smacked him alongside his head with a wooden spoon. "Ya idiot! I can't believe I'm related to you. I said knock her off...not knock her out! Ya put the wrong stuff in the dessert. And that woman ain't Amy Claiborne! You da most incredibly stupid.....!"

Tommy ran for the back door leading to the Alley with Bubba right behind him smacking him about the head.

Amy started feeling fine as soon as they left Brennan's. "Sorry, I don't know what happened to me."

"Let's sit for a second. My nerves could do with a rest. I don't know what Marie would do to me if anything happened to you."

"That's so silly. What could possibly happen to me?"

They sat across the street from the restaurant on beautifully carved concrete benches.

It was only a matter of minutes before an ambulance and two police cars careened around the corner and pulled up in front of Brennan's.

"What's going on?"

Recognizing the young couple coming out on the stretchers, Jimmy raced across the street and listened to the medics in the ambulance before returning to Amy.

"They're okay. Two tourists. They're sitting up and talking. Must have been out in the sun too long. They'll be okay."

"Are you sure?"

"I'll find out. My brother Liam works in the kitchen. He'll tell me what happened. Right now let's get going."

"Well?" Seamus demanded when Bubba scrambled up the concrete bench and sat nervously twitching beside him. "What is wrong with ye?"

"There was a little tiny glitch, cher."

Seamus wanted to explode but he had to keep his temper in check. He needed these stupid rat people. "Like what?"

"Well, ma brother Tommy accidentally put the wrong thing in the Bananas Foster which is this really tasty----"

"Is she dead or alive?"

"Ohhhh...dead or alive...do we have to get so philosophical?"

Bubba shrank into the bench when he saw the look of hatred Seamus was giving him.

"You're the stupidest rats I've ever run into."

"We are not rats. We are Cajuns in a very unfortunate and temporary, very, very temporary situation... let me hasten to add...only for the time being, and—"

"---You're stupid Cajun rats. I can do better on my own." He smashed his rolled up newspaper against the concrete bench right where Bubba had been sitting.

Bubba ran for his life.

Seamus ran after the Cajun rat but quickly lost him in the maze of narrow streets in the French Quarter. He ended up in front of Lafitte's Blacksmith Shop, built in circa 1772, according to its sign. Seamus went inside the dark bar lit only with candles and a blazing fire in the fireplace. Someone was playing soft blues on a piano in the far corner. A sign behind the bar on the wall said "I love Ireland."

Taking a seat at the well worn mahogany bar Seamus swiveled his barstool and rested his elbows on the bar behind him. There were a few patrons eating and drinking at two of the tables. He figured it was still early for the early starters and too late for the late night crowd.

"Can I get ye something?" A red headed giant of a man stood behind the bar wiping a glass.

"A dark ale for start. Ye're from Ireland?"

"Aye. Name's Angus Finlay." The bartender poured out a beer from a tap and placed it in front of his only customer. All the tourists were out at the parades but soon they would come through the doors thirsty, hungry and tired, looking for a place to sit and a strong brew to drink.

"Seamus Flynn. Originally from Craigmore."

"I know the place well. Lived in Clagton." Angus rinsed out a glass and dried it.

"Small world."

"Tis indeed. How do ye like Mardi Gras...is it ye first time?"

"Aye, 'tis."

"The big crowds are at the parades. They'll come strollin' in here about an hour."

"Too many people for me. Didn't expect that."

"Gets worse, too. On Fat Tuesday, I stay home an' watch it on TV."

"This place is called Lafitte's. Does it have anything to do with the pirate Jean Lafitte?"

"It does indeed. Lafitte built this tavern with secret tunnels below the street to haul goods from his ships to sell tax free. Everything came through here an' his hotel."

"Hotel?"

"The Golden Palace. One street over towards the River, middle of the block. If ye blink ye'll miss it. I know the night manager. Good friend of mine. If ye want to stay there after Mardi Gras ends let me know."

"Is it true there's a Pirates Ball on the night of Mardi Gras?"

"It's a ball like no other. It's said they're real pirates but it's really just a bunch of bankers. They're the

<u>real</u> pirates." The bartender laughed and slapped the counter with a wiping cloth.

"What happens at one of these balls? I've never been to one."

"Well, there's a parade made up with a bunch of trucks fancied up with decorations and stuff. There are people riding on the truck, they are called krewe members, who throw doubloons and beads and stuff. Then the king of the parade stops his truck at City Hall and he toasts his queen. Then he goes on to the auditorium, that's just a few blocks from here in the French Quarter. His queen is taken by fancy limo from City Hall to join him. An' then they have a really big party there with everyone from the trucks and lots of invited guests.

"I think I'd like to splurge an' get a limo for my big day. I leave the day after Mardi Gras. What limo company drives the queen? I want the best."

"Magee Limos. I even know the Queen's driver for the big night."

"I'd like to meet the fellow. He might drive me around for a day or two."

"That would be good business for Mickey Daly. I'll just write his number down for ye."

Seamus pocketed the written number. This was very good information for sure. "Got to go. I'll be back."

"I can get ye an invite for one of the balls. Ye let me know."

"Thanks. Do you think you could get me into this Pirates Ball?"

"I'll do me best."

Seamus quickly walked back to his bench in Jackson Square. He hoped Amy would be coming back that way.

"Where to now? My feet hurt. Can we stop for a bit?"

"No time. We have one thing left to do for the ball. We have to get your throws. Those are little trinkets like doubloons and carnival beads that you'll throw to the crowd when you're on the top porch at City Hall. Then we'll go back in three days for the final gown fitting and you are ready to go."

"I think that will make Marie happy."

"I _know_ that will make Marie happy."

They were passing by The Sweet Shop, a place Amy was getting to know in the French Quarter. She waved to the owner, Suzie, who was arranging a large basket of sweet treats in the window.

"Look at these fantastic candies!" She stopped.

"We'll stop and talk to Suzie another time but right now we—"

"---Jimmy, you've got to see this!"

Jimmy was already walking down the street. They were never going to finish all the parade chores at this rate.

"Amy, we don't have time right now. After we finish our chores we can come back."

Amy was very interested in a large poster in the window on prominent display.

"It says there's going to be a Murder Mystery Dinner Party at one of the most famous haunted plantations in Louisiana. Do you know The Devereux Plantation on River Road?"

"Of course. In the 1850s it was the biggest supplier of sugar in Louisiana. They had acres of sugar cane in production. A few years ago Mary Devereux turned it into a Bed & Breakfast. Suzie, the owner of The Sweet Shop is her cousin."

"It's Saturday night. Could we go, Jimmy? Please. I've always wanted to visit a haunted plantation and to participate in a Murder Mystery Dinner Party would be perfect. Please, Jimmy. Say you'll take me there."

"Look, I'll give Suzie a call later and make the arrangements."

"I won't budge until you make the arrangements now."

Jimmy knew the stubborn look on Amy's face meant they weren't going anywhere until he did.

"Oh, all right. But I'm going to add bossy to your list of giant character flaws!"

"Okay."

Amy followed Jimmy into the store.

"Hi Suzie. We would like to go to the Murder Mystery Dinner Party tomorrow night. Is it too late to get two reservations?"

"I'll call Mary, right away." She talked while she waited for Mary to answer the phone. " You're Amy. Your Mom used to come into my shop all the time. She especially loved the pralines." Completing her call she hung up. "You are all set."

Suzie reached into a basket on the counter and handed Amy two large cellophane and ribbon wrapped pralines. "On the house." They were a creamy shade of light brown with nuts poking through the sugary coating.

"Thank you. I'd love to come back and talk to you sometime. And I'm really looking forward to see the Devereux plantation. I've read about it." Amy smiled while Suzie handed the tickets to Amy and Jimmy paid the tab. Grumbling he took Amy's arm and rushed her towards the door.

"I think you'll have a wonderful time. Mary and her sister, Delia, are famous for their Murder Mystery parties."

Amy called back over her shoulder. "Wonderful and I know I will love these pralines, too."

She gave one to Jimmy and put the other in her pocket for later.

""You didn't have to rush me out of there! Where is this plantation?"

"A few hours drive from here."

"How will we get there?"

"I'll check with Mickey Daly. He's going to be your limo driver for the Ball. Maybe he has time to take us."

Amy leaned down and kissed the top of Jimmy's head. "Thank you."

Jimmy blushed the color of his red velvet pants and hoped she didn't see.

Amy started making plans for the trip. "I've never been to a Murder Mystery Dinner Party. And a haunted plantation! This is very exciting. Although I did read that Devereux is one of the magnificent plantations in Louisiana I didn't know it's a Bed & Breakfast, too. Do we stay the night or come home?"

"Are you crazy? Marie would be furious if you were out of the house for an entire night so close to the ball. You know how important it is that you reign as Queen of the Pirates Ball Tuesday night?"

"Why don't you tell me all about the Ball?"

"Let's talk as we walk."

"I won't move a step until you say we can go to that Murder Mystery Dinner Party with or without Mr. Daly and his car. What if he's busy? We could take a taxi...or a carriage."

Jimmy didn't mention that the cost of a taxi would be out of sight nor the time it would take for a carriage to get there.

"I'll call Mickey. I can't guarantee anything."

"Will you try?"

"Yessss!"

Seamus couldn't believe his great luck when he watched Amy stop in front of the window of the sweet shop. She was reading something with great interest. It must have been very exciting since she was clapping her hands and smiling.

They went inside the store and when they came out they rushed off down the street.

Seamus was torn between following them or going to see what was in the window of the shop. He was glad he went to see what was so fascinating. It was an announcement for a Murder Mystery Dinner Party at some plantation tomorrow night. So that's what the excitement was all about. Something like that would definitely appeal to Amy.

Seamus pulled out his cell phone and called the number on the poster. It was easy to secure a reservation, under the name John Billings, for the Murder Mystery

Dinner Party. Just in case he needed one he made a reservation for staying the night, too. The owner of Devereux Plantation told him she was delighted to have so many interested guests. After all it was the weekend before Mardi Gras and she had expected everyone would be staying in New Orleans for the parades.

He had no idea what a Murder Mystery Dinner Party was but his friend Angus would know. He headed back to the Lafitte Tavern.

Bubba and two of his rat brothers had been watching from the park across the street. As soon as Seamus left, they scurried over, read the poster in the sweet shop window and started making their own plans.

Amy almost ran into Jimmy when he stopped in front of a shop with a small "Mardi Gras Throws" sign. They went through the door into a magical place with beads, doubloons, baskets of gilded coconuts, feather masks and a variety of necklaces with plastic alligators, shiny red crawfish and brightly colored Mississippi River Steamboats.

Jimmy had a basket and was rushing up and down the aisles gathering strands of multi- colored pearls, beads in colors of purple, gold and green.

Amy was fascinated with the gilded coconuts.

"Put those back. They're for the krewes on the Zulu floats."

"Oh. Yes. I read all about the famous Zulu parades."

"You are the Queen of the Pirates Ball. You'll be throwing pirate beads and little treasures from the balcony at City Hall the night of the parade. Did you know the pirates from Treasure Island will be in the ball? They told Michael that you are a treasure better than gold and jewels and they can't wait to see you reign as the Pirate Queen."

"That was really sweet of them to say that." Amy dropped the gilded coconuts back into the reed basket with the others. "Remember you said you'd tell me all about what I had to do."

"Later...later. After we get everything I have a surprise for you."

"What is it!"

"Only if you let me finish what I have to do."

Amy smiled. "If I can help in any way, do let me

know." "Just another ten minutes." "Okay."

Amy wandered up and down the aisles while Jimmy raced around like a whirlwind gathering everything on his list and then standing impatiently in line. He arranged for everything to be delivered to Marie at the house.

"We have nothing more to do until the final dress fitting Tuesday morning so we can now have fun."

"Tell me about the surprise!"

"We're going on a special boat in Pirate Village. We'll go up sand dunes, through caves, under the water...oh everywhere...wait and see."

Amy was jumping up and down and clapping even as they passed through a wall into Pirate Village. Jimmy flagged down a carriage.

A huge pirate ship with a glass lid was rocking gently in the harbor. Riders were boarding and taking their assigned seats. She guessed Jimmy had called ahead since they were waved through and seated in the front row where they had the very best view.

The ship quickly filled with riders and the glass lid closed with a loud bang, snapping shut securely. Amy held on to her seat with arms almost as frozen as her smile.

The sails were furled and the ship was underway only a few minutes when they suddenly saw a sand bar that kept building and building. The ship sailed up to the top of the sand mountain and then careened down the other side through an entrance into a stone cave that materialized out of nowhere.

The inside of the cave was dark and cold. The pirate ship flew through the air. Everyone behind Amy was screaming in excitement. The cave went on for what seemed like forever. There were sudden twists and turns and once the ship listed so far on its left side that she thought they were going to flip over and sink into the turquoise lagoon below. The ship righted itself and everyone gave a sigh of relief and then they were up and down and all around.

Amy could see a bright spot of blue sky at the end of the long tunnel. The ship shot ahead aiming for the ever widening opening and at the last minute it flew out bow first and plunged under the water.

It was incredibly beautiful under the sea. A variety of fish in all the colors of an artist palette swam by bumping their heads against the glass. Amy was so enchanted with the view she didn't have a second to be afraid. An octopus smacked against the glass near her seat and held on with its tentacles. A shark swam by followed by a school of silver barracuda with their nasty teeth making them look like they were smiling. Colorful man-of-war jellyfish pulsed through the water in formation.

The ship had sunk far down to the sandy bottom. Amy looked out the windows and could see treasure chests full of gold and silver bars. Brightly colored jewels were strewn about the white sand around the chests. Rubies, emeralds, and diamonds glittered in the filtered sunlight. A battered pirate ship had sunk nearby with its timbers rotting and its cannons thrown here and there.

Amy felt a drizzle of water touch her head and shoulders. "Jimmy, is it supposed to rain inside?"

Jimmy looked at her in horror. "Don't worry. Just a little malfunction."

He stood and motioned to the tour guide to come over. "Ahhh...I was wondering—" Before he had a chance to finish his sentence the tour guide started screaming in a very high pitched voice.

"Don't panic, everyone! We have a leak! Don't panic!" There was nowhere to go. They were trapped in the bottom of the lagoon in a ship that was now leaking water like a waterfall. It could be said they were going to sink but they were already on the bottom.

"Jimmy, do something!"

"I can't."

"What?"

"I have no powers underwater. It sort of blots it out."

"Well try! We're going to drown if you don't try!"

Jimmy pulled out glittering gold dust out of his pocket and threw it in the air.

The Black Witch was drawn outside to her courtyard, a lush garden with delicate ferns and tropical flowers. The smell of gardenias and night blooming jasmine filled the air. Giant Magnolia Trees and Bird of Paradise soared high against the stone walls surrounding the courtyard, giving the house total privacy. But today a threat of a rain storm turned the air heavy with moisture. Bolts of black lightning flashed over the pond in the center of the yard. She drew a crystal ball from the folds of her robe. Holding it up she gazed into its depths.

Serena clutched her chest in agony. Her precious Amy was in Pirate Village in a ship at the bottom of the lagoon and it was taking in water. Who would dare to hurt a child she loved above all, the daughter of her son. She threw her head back and waved her arms into the wind. "Protect her now and keep her safe.
Let no hand cause her harm.
Or they will wish they had not been born."

At once the leak in the ship repaired itself and the ship rose from the bottom of the lagoon like Poseidon rising from the ocean.

"Show me who dares threaten my beloved child."

Like a silent movie the images unfolded in the crystal ball. The ship was old. The cracks, the leaks, the stress of age. It was no one's fault. An accident.
"Repair yourself like a child newborn
and never let anyone come to harm."

With a wave of her hands the ship was once again like new. The years of use fell away. By the time the Pirate Ship got back to the dock, the owners would be in shock over the changes. She smiled.

The sky cleared. It was a pleasant evening to sit outside with, Annie, a Jack Russell mix puppy she'd found abandoned on her doorstep many years ago and now was her constant companion.

Annie bent over her water bowl and began to drink. Serena loved that sound. Annie drank with such gusto. She smiled. "I miss Monsieur Monkey." Annie spoke in a whisper of sadness.

Serena reached down and patted Annie's head. "I do, too."

She thought of the curious little monkey who loved to swing by his tail in the tall trees in the courtyard. On exceptionally beautiful days he loved entertain French Quarter visitors swinging by his tail from the wrought iron railing on the fourth floor. On just such a day he saw Miss Suzette, a beautiful little female monkey that worked in a circus that was passing through town. He ran off to join the circus and be with his true love. Annie missed him dearly.

"I wish I had a tail so I could swing in the trees."

"Would you stay off the balconies? I couldn't bear it if you ran off with some handsome little french poodle passing by."

"I promise! I promise! I will never leave. You saved me. I will never forget your kindness to me."

Annie was beside herself with joy. It would be a dream to be so free.

The Black Witch clicked her fingers. How could she deny anything to someone so precious to her? "Now you have a monkey tail. Use it wisely."

Annie raced up the tree barking with joy.

The Black Witch loved making her friend so happy.

When they returned to the dock Amy couldn't praise Jimmy enough for saving the ship and everyone aboard. Jimmy knew it wasn't by his hand. There was only one person who had that kind of power.

Although Jimmy wondered if the connection between Amy and the Black Witch was really true, he was relieved that Amy was now under her protection.

After accepting future free tickets and praise for their quick thinking from the Captain of the Undersea Pirate Ship ride, Jimmy took Amy's arm and hurried off.

Catching a passing carriage Jimmy quickly got them settled before turning to Amy. "How would you like to go to visit that shop that had that The Pirate Treasure Game in the window?"

"I would love that!"

Giving the driver the directions they sat back and enjoyed a vision of shops and cafes that passed in a rush.

"What is that wonderful smell?"

"Fried alligator."

Amy shrank back in her seat. "Ohh...is it really good?"

"Tastes like chicken." Jimmy slapped his knee and laughed.

There was a huge crowd in front of the Pirate Gift shop front window. After a long wait, Amy and Jimmy finally had a front row view.

"That's The Pirate Treasure Game. I have a huge one set up in my dining room!"

Model versions of pirate ships were milling about in a small lake in the window. Amy spotted the name "Queen Anne's Revenge" on one. She knew that was Blackbeard's ship. "The Adventure Galley" was Captain Kidd's ship. Suddenly Kidd's ship fired something that looked like a skunk with goggles at Blackbeard's ship and the battle was on. Amy blinked her eyes. Did she really see a gang of skunks with goggles shot out of the cannons?

They managed to squeeze inside the shop but it was filled with cannon smoke, lake water splashing all around, and boys of all ages yelling and cheering on their favorite pirate captain.

"Let's get out of here. It's getting late and it would be wise to get you home and talk to Marie. Let me do the talking."

"Good idea." Amy raced ahead of him out the door.

"If all goes well then I'll meet you in the morning and take you to Leprechaun City." Jimmy put a finger up to his lips. "Then later we'll go to the Murder Mystery thing."

"I was wondering if ye might give me a ride to a plantation tomorrow night? I signed up for a Murder Mystery Dinner Party. I tried calling Mickey but the limo office said he was booked up until after Mardi Gras."

Angus laughed. "I can. But Seamus, are ye sure ye want to go. Ye're gonna miss a big parade tomorrow night. Saturday is one of the biggest days except for Fat Tuesday."

"I've seen me share of parades but I've never been to a dinner like that."

"Do ye have the directions to this place?"

"The Devereux Plantation on River Road. Do ye know of it?

"Sure as I do. Said to be haunted."

"Might see a ghost or two if I'm lucky."

"I kin drop ye off and visit some friends in the area. Ye can call me on me cell phone and I'll come back for ye."

"Thank ye, Angus. I'm lucky to have met ye."

"Luck of the Irish...I'm sure. Ye will have to tell me all about it. Be here tomorrow between four and five. It's a good one hour drive."

"Thank ye. See ye tomorrow."

Seamus left whistling a tune. He missed seeing his former Cajun rat friend crouched in a dark corner listening to what was going on before Bubba squeezed back through the hole between the floor molding and the ancient brick floor.

CHAPTER SIX
Playing The Pirate Treasure Game

As usual, the French Quarter was packed with tourists so Jimmy took Amy to the hidden tunnel in the garden of The Golden Palace that would lead them back to the Claiborne family home.

Marie was waiting for them as usual, sitting in Celeste's favorite chair. At least they were back before dark.

"Marie, we had the dress fitting, we bought all the throws that will be delivered to you tomorrow and we went on a Pirate Ship ride and we had a marvelous day." Jimmy rushed to tell her in one long breath.

"You mean the Bayou Ride?"

Amy clapped her hands and laughed. "No, the one that goes under the water and through the wonderful cave—"

"—under the water!" Marie was almost in shock. "Jimmy, I told you nothing dangerous!"

"But Marie...it wasn't dangerous at all. Jimmy threw out his gold dust when we sprang a leak sitting on the bottom of the lagoon and we rose to the surface immediately. There is nothing Jimmy can't do. He's wonderful, Marie, honestly!"

Marie stared daggers at Jimmy who averted his eyes. She knew all too well that Jimmy's magical gold dust didn't work underwater. She knew there was only one person who had that kind of power. But Marie didn't have to wonder why the Black Witch was Amy's protector. Marie knew that Celeste had run off with Philippe, the son of the Black Witch and that Amy was her granddaughter.

"Marie, tomorrow we are going—"

Jimmy cut her off. "We're going to my house. I'm going to show Amy The Pirate Treasure Game."

"I am very relieved to hear that you two will be inside tomorrow. There is a huge storm headed this way. The weather channel said it's due in the late afternoon with a cold front behind it. So be sure you stay inside."

"Don't worry about us."

Amy wondered why Jimmy didn't mention the Murder Mystery Dinner Party but then she knew it was probably because Marie would say she couldn't go. And she really wanted to go.

"Amy, you look exhausted. Why don't you sleep late and ring for Glory when you wake up. She'll bring your breakfast to your room. Jimmy, off with you. Glory will let me know when Amy is up and I'll give you a call."

With a tip of his hat he disappeared through the secret door locking it behind him.

"I left a plate of sandwiches and a thermos of warm milk on your bedside table. Just leave the tray in the hall when you're finished. Glory will be along to pick it up."

"Thank you, Marie. You think of everything."

"I know Jimmy and I'm sure he kept you moving at a fast pace with nothing to eat."

Marie left Amy alone to get ready for bed. She really was very tired. But not too tired to finish the small plate of lovely ham and turkey finger sandwiches resting over a bed of ice and a glass of warm milk. Just the thing for making one very sleepy.

She remembered her praline but she was too full to eat anything more. She put it in the top drawer of her bedside table.

Her hand brushed a small indentation in the back of the drawer. She wondered what it was. Was this one of the secret places Marie had told her about? She pushed it in and heard a clicking noise. A little trap door popped open.

Amy carefully lifted out a folded note. Beautiful handwriting in black ink, now faded with time, filled the cream colored stationery.

"My Darling Serena, I built a house for us and returned to surprise you but you were gone. Cook told me you had married someone and left with him. Why? I am returning now to the island home in the Caribbean that was to be a surprise for you with a broken heart. There will never be anyone for me but you. I will love you forever. Lafitte."

This love note must have been written in the early 1800s, she thought. Tomorrow she would ask Marie or Jimmy. And who was Serena?

She remembered to put the tray outside her door in the hallway before climbing into the soft bed.

In no time Amy was fast asleep.

Amy woke up well past breakfast the next morning. She was clutching the green jade heart in her hand. Every time she touched it she felt it grow warm, which was very strange indeed.

Far away in a fishing village on the coast of France a woman who was teaching a class in French to a small group of village children was suddenly thinking about a young girl only three years old. She could see the girl disappearing in the mist. She could hear her own voice crying out. "Be my brave little girl." She was told Amy and all the children had drowned.

"Madame Celeste? Are you alright?"

"Yes, thank you, Angeline. Now where were we?"

Amy pulled on the embroidered sash by her bed and just as she finished putting on her robe and slippers Glory was at her door with a tray piled with wonderful things to eat. There were soft boiled eggs in small silver cups, tiny triangles of toast she called little soldiers, hot chocolate in a special chocolate pot, and crispy fried little pillows of dough, hollow inside and covered with powdered sugar.

Just as she was about to take a bite Glory said "When eating beignets don't breathe in or out or you'll be covered in white powdered sugar. Breathe after you put it down."

Amy laughed and did what she suggested. She didn't want to be covered with sugar on such a wonderful day like today. She couldn't wait to play the pirate game and then on to visit a haunted plantation. This was something she had only read about in books.

After she finished breakfast she thought carefully about what she was going to wear. Thanks to Marie there were new outfits in the armoire in her room every day. Hanging up were cashmere dresses, the finest wool pants and silk blouses. She chose from her newest outfits. Today she would wear a black silk shirt and layer in with a black pullover sweater. Then black wool slacks. Everything she was going to wear would work well day and night. She dressed quickly. She remembered to put the love note she found the night before in the pocket of her slacks.

The apple green jade heart stood out against the black of her sweater. Since the day was both cold and rainy a wool lined raincoat made sense and would not arouse any suspicion in Marie.

Amy put the tray outside her door and pulled the sash by her bed. In a few minutes she could hear Marie talking to Glory and the tray was quickly picked up.

Marie knocked and entered, surprised to see Amy ready for the day ahead. "I will call Jimmy. The Pirate Treasure Game is great fun and Jimmy has the very best one."

"We saw it in the window of the gift shop but there was such a crowd!"

"I am sure Jimmy has rounded up his brothers to play the game with you. I'll call him. He'll come by way of the tunnel. The weather is already terrible outside. The winds are fierce. But it will all clear out in a few hours so don't worry."

"Thank you, Marie."

"You are safe with Jimmy."

Marie left so fast Amy forgot to mention the love letter.

It wasn't long after Marie left that Jimmy clicked open the secret door by the side of the fireplace and appeared with a big smile and "Top of the mornin' to you!"

"I am really excited about playing that pirate game."

"Well then, let's go."

Amy followed Jimmy through the secret door. They turned right and headed down a flight of stairs. Lit torches, secured against the tunnel walls, gave them ample light to see where they were going although Amy was sure Jimmy could find the way with his eyes closed.

The tunnel ended in a blank wall. Jimmy threw out some gold dust and a door appeared. They entered the first room that led to a line of rooms off a central hallway. She might have expected magical harps played by garden fairies and golden singing birds in silver cages. Instead the great room held a blazing fireplace and heavy ancient wood beams running with the length of the low ceiling. It looked like one of the wayside English taverns she had read about in historical romance novels.

"Jimmy, this room is warm and welcoming."

"Reminds me of home in Ireland."

At that three younger versions of Jimmy came tumbling into the room.

"These are my brothers. This is Liam. He works for the restaurant where we had that memorable brunch...remember?"

"I do indeed. Hello, Liam."

Liam blushed.

"This is Paddy. He works at the library in the French Quarter."

"Paddy, I adore libraries. We had a wonderful library at St. Luke's."

Paddy smiled and handed her a book titled, "The Bayou Pirates."

"Thank you, Paddy. I haven't read this one. I love anything to do with pirates."

Paddy's cheeks turned red.

"And this is Danny, the youngest."

Danny took his headphones off and waved.

"Danny wants to be on one of those singing shows he sees on TV."

"Very nice meeting you, Danny. Maybe you'll sing for me sometime."

Danny was overwhelmed with joy. Someone who took him seriously was a friend forever.

"Set up the game board, boys. Amy is here to play."

The boys hooped and yelled in excitement as they raced out of the room.

"It's a board game? But we saw the pirate ships on a small lake firing at one another yesterday. And Jimmy I meant to ask you about the skunks?

"It's too horrible outside to play on the lake. Look..."

Jimmy snapped his fingers and forest green velvet drapes opened revealing a huge floor to ceiling window with a view of a large body of water. Amy was amazed that since they were underground, where did the open ocean of water came from as pirate ships, under full sail, heaved up and down in the rough seas. Heavy black clouds hung low in the sky while enormous waves crashed on the decks and driving rain pelted the windows of the ships in a fury.

"We can play it outside another day, when it's warm and sunny."

"Okay." Nothing about Jimmy surprised her anymore.

"This way." Jimmy led Amy into the large game room.

The brothers were rushing about setting up the board on a round dining room table that could seat twelve. There were overstuffed chairs for everyone to sit in.

"It's very easy---" Paddy started to explain.

Amy studied the intricate schooner tokens.

"There are forts and ships. We each choose a Fort."

"Paddy, what if we are five players, like today?" "No problem. Watch. Five players, please!"

The board came rumbling to life splashing water all over the place and yelling in a big booming voice, "Make up ye mind o' there be consequences!"

The ports rearranged themselves for five players.

Amy whispered to Danny, "What consequences?"

Danny grinned and whispered back, "He's just a big puff of wind. Don't mind the Captain."

"I heard that!" The waves perked up and hovered in Danny's direction like a huge dark grey hand waiting to crash over the young boy.

"Just a little youthful exuberance. Take no harm." Jimmy spoke quickly while giving Danny the evil eye that said he better behave.

The board grumbled back to normal.

At the bottom of the newly arranged board was Fort New Orleans.

"I want Fort New Orleans!" Amy clapped her hands. She slipped the pirate book Paddy had given her into the pocket of her coat.

The game board fit the table perfectly. She sat down in front of Fort New Orleans. To her left, going clockwise, was Fort Key West, then further on was Fort Bahamas. Then came Fort Jamaica and Fort Bermuda which made up the five points on the board. Each fort had a pirate Captain and his ship. In order...Jean Lafitte, Sir Francis Drake, Henry Morgan, The fierce Blackbeard, and Bartholomew Roberts knows as Black Bart.

Everyone had their own Fort with their own token Pirate Ship.

Amy could see Paddy was gearing up to teach her the game but she had watched the game played in the window of the Pirate Gift shop and Jimmy had told her a lot about the game, too. Not wanting to hurt his feelings she let him explain.

"You're the Captain. You make the decisions on your pirate ship. You start out with a treasure chest and twenty gold pieces of eight. You can use your gold to buy things. Oh, you'll see as we play."

Danny, eager to get the game started, jumped in and said, "You roll the dice and your ship sails clockwise on the board, in nautical miles, the amount on the dice. There are twenty nautical miles from one fort to the next. The Captain who goes around the board and comes back to his home port without sinking in a hurricane or being snatched out of the water by a giant sea monster lurking in the depths, is the winner."

Liam had to have his say, "And of course, the Captain who gets back to his home port, has to have the most gold, silver and jewels taken from the other ships or find the loot on tropical islands by following ancient treasure maps—"

"---Or diving for sunken treasures of the deep." Danny added enthusiastically.

Liam continued, "Yes, and as you go around the board you will sometimes land on places that tell you to open the Treasure Box which will have either a treasure or something awful or some direction for you to follow, good or bad."

"You are our guest so you roll first." Liam handed Amy the dice and jumped up. "I am last so I'll see to the snacks."

"Quite the chef, he is."

Amy saw the pride Jimmy had in his brothers.

"Let me take your coat." Danny held out his arms. Amy tried not to laugh when Danny, being the youngest of the brothers, struggled off, barely able to see over her coat and sweater.

"Here goes."

Amy rolled a four and a two. She moved her pirate ship six spaces and landed on a square that spoke loudly and said, "Go to the Treasure Box and collect your bounty."

"Bounty?" Amy laughed.

"Open and see what you have!" Screamed the treasure box.

Amy opened the box and a card flew out, landing in her hand.

"Pick out six skunks and six cannons. Good luck and SHUT MY LID!" The box screamed out again.

Quickly shutting the box Amy turned the card over to see if there was anything else.

Paddy, the self appointed teacher of the game explained. "The skunks are the ammo for the cannons. There is absolute chaos when the crew of the other pirate ship sees six skunks with very determined expressions, wearing goggles, flying leather caps and white silk scarves, shoot out of the cannons and land on their deck making that terrible skunk smell. I've seen an entire crew jump in the water. Then you can overtake them and get all the pirate treasure they've collected! And you can do it with ease."

"What happens to the crew?"

"After you take all the treasure then they are allowed to take back their ship." Jimmy explained.

"What about their food?"

"Nah. We leave them food." Liam smiled. "Unless...they have any tins of French pate or escargots then we take that, too."

"Escargot?" Danny looked intrigued.

"Snails."

"Ewwww!" Danny made a face.

"Don't ewww it unless you try it." Liam said. "The snails are farm raised and then sautéed in butter, garlic and parsley. They are fantastic. Oh, and with French bread to dip in the butter garlic sauce."

Amy laughed. "Oh, skunks! How funny! And now I can't wait to try and make these escargot!"

"Liam works for Brennan's, a famous restaurant in the French Quarter. Maybe you would like to make escargot with him sometime."

Amy clapped her hands. "Liam, I love to cook. I helped out in the kitchen at the Orphanage..." At that moment Amy remembered Mrs. Richardson saying 'Don't cook for anyone, Amy, at least not anyone who is going to eat what you cook.' "Liam, you could teach me how to be a really great cook."

"I'd love to."

"Well!" The treasure box shouted impatiently.

"Well what?"

"Pick your skunks!" The box ordered.

The card jumped out of her hand and did a little dance on the table until Amy grabbed it, sticking it under the board in front of her.

A bleacher like the kind you see at baseball games appeared in the middle of the table filled with cheering skunks all yelling "Pick me! Pick me!" which was really funny since they all looked alike. They frantically waved their paws in the air bumping each other out of the way.

"You have to pick six skunks. Your choice."

Amy talked to the little enthusiastic skunks. "I am so sorry I can only pick six of you. It's so unfair since you are all great. I'll take the six from the front row."

The six little skunks chosen jumped up cheering and quickly climbed into Amy's treasure chest, pulling the lid shut. The rest of the unpicked bunch in the bleachers sadly lowered their little paws then disappeared in a poof of smoke.

"PHEW!" The treasure box loudly shut his lid.

Danny patted her hand. "Romeo can be a bit irritable at times. We just overlook his little faults."

Amy started to giggle. She was playing a board game with Romeo, a talking treasure box, and flying skunks wearing goggles that were shot out of cannons. Liam was going to teach her how to cook snails!

Jimmy was next and left Fort Key West for the Bahamas. He traveled eight miles, landing on a square that loudly told him to go back to his home port.

Jimmy laughed. "Better now at the start then later at the end!"

Danny, with youthful exuberance, was full of energy. He was up, down, and all around the table holding the huge game board.

Amy noticed that the board was well worn. She could see the edge worn in front of Paddy where he rested his elbow holding up his chin while he was deep in thought. And there were finger marks on the board in front of Danny where he held on in great excitement waiting to hear what his fate would be from the Treasure Box. In front of Liam was a part of the board where you could see little oil spots. It was where Liam was stirring some good thing he brought in a bowl from the kitchen in between his plays. Only the board in front of Jimmy and her own place were not marked. Amy knew at once that they most of the time they were four ports, four players.

Jimmy the oldest, with one smile, kept his brothers in line.

Amy felt more at home here than when she was at her Aunt Lily's big house on Royal Street.

Danny's pirate ship landed on a spot that told him, in a very mysterious tone of voice, to open the Treasure Box. A card popped out and the box said, in a still irritated voice, "You have found a message in a bottle, floating in the ocean. Read what's written and tell us what you want to do."

Out of nowhere a glass bottle, dripping wet, materialized in Danny's hand.

Danny yanked out the cork and pulled a very old parchment from the bottle that he unfurled at once and studied intently.

"It's Blackbeard's treasure map! Wow! I'm going to search for Blackbeard's treasure!" Danny couldn't sit still.

Liam laughed. "Remember when I spent all afternoon looking for Lafitte's treasure in the bayou from a map in a bottle like that one?"

Danny gave his brother a disapproving look and with a snap of his fingers Danny and the map disappeared.

"Where did he go?" Amy was amazed.

"He'll be back before his next turn. He's off looking for the treasure."

Danny was thrilled at the prospect of his pirate treasure map being the real thing and he might come back with diamonds, rubies and gold that he could add to his treasure chest.

He landed on a small deserted island near Fort Jamaica. He could see Blackbeard's pirate ship, "The Queen Anne's Revenge" at anchor, bobbing up and down in the water.

A rowdy group of pirates were partying on the top deck.

Hoping he was alone on the island, but just in case, he moved silently through the palm trees. He didn't want to run into any of Blackbeard's men and definitely not Blackbeard himself. He knew that the infamous pirate captain was a huge man, near six feet five inches tall. When he went into battle he would set off sparklers woven into his long black beard giving the impression that his face was on fire. He terrified most of his opponents and they gave up their ships willingly and handed over all their treasure to him. Blackbeard's buried treasure was a fact but just <u>where</u> it was buried no one knew. And now Danny had a chance to find one of the famous pirates many buried chests.

He carefully followed the directions on the map. He found the whispering tree with the two headed snake wrapped around the trunk three feet above the tentacle of roots. He paced 50 steps South towards a waterfall that fell upside down into a pond. Carefully making his way behind the waterfall he entered the cave whose walls were shining with what looked like gold which he knew was fool's gold because only a fool would think it was real. Water trickled down the walls of the cave making it very humid inside.

The last direction on the map told him to look for the treasure chest to be behind a rock formation on his right that looked like a pyramid. He finally found it.

The lock was rusted on the old wooden chest. Danny had to bash it a bit with stones lying on the ground but it finally popped open revealing.....nothing! It was empty!

Danny didn't have time to think about his bad luck since he heard cannons firing from Blackbeard's ship.

He raced to the cave entrance and saw a group of the pirates heading for the waterfall. He ducked to one side and stayed very still. He wanted to disappear but his magic powder didn't work in the presence of water so he closed his eyes and hoped they wouldn't see him.

The pirates didn't get as far as the cave. They were too busy bathing in the pond below the upside down waterfall.

The minute they left Danny raced out making his way into the trees. Once away from water he threw out his powder and disappeared. He hadn't found the treasure but he had an incredible story to tell about his adventure.

Danny enchanted Amy with his story about the waterfall and the pirates. His brothers just rolled their eyes and kept teasing him because he didn't find the treasure. He finally had such a gloomy look on his face, Amy laughed.

"Oh, no, Danny, what's important is it was a really great adventure. Sometimes the most fun is in getting there."

This cheered him up considerably. He liked Amy a lot.

Liam rolled next and won a chance at the Treasure Box that gave him three large bags of bees.

Amy laughed.

"They're the best. You shoot them out of the cannons and when they land on the other ship's deck the bag breaks open and they sting everything in sight. I've even seen the ship's dog leap over the side."

"I love this game!" Amy ruffled Danny's hair while Danny gazed at her with adoration.

They played all afternoon.

Amy didn't want to stop but it was already four o'clock and their driver, Mickey, was waiting to take them to the Devereux Plantation for the Murder Mystery Dinner Party.

"The great thing about this game is that we can leave it right here and start again when you come back to visit." Paddy explained.

Danny retrieved her coat from a hall closet. Amy promised to tell the brothers all about the haunted plantation the next time she visited, which she said would be very soon.

Danny took her hand while they walked through the Great Room.

Amy leaned down and kissed the top of Danny's head.

Danny spun around twice and did a small cartwheel.

"I think you won his heart." Jimmy smiled and opened the door to the tunnel.

A very strange looking woman stood there taking up the entire doorway. Amy was tall but this woman was at least one foot taller and a few feet wider.

She was wearing a long gown of silk velvet patches in vibrant colors. She had a black lace shawl around her shoulders and a black lace cap on her head. Red corkscrew curls sneaked out from the side and back of a lace cap giving her a very madcap look indeed.

She lowered her wire framed eyeglasses with a hand wearing a black lace fingerless glove.

"Just in time for tea, I am!"

Amy, Queen of the Pirates Ball

CHAPTER SEVEN
A Murder Mystery Dinner Party

"Aunt Maggie!" Jimmy, in speechless surprise, backed up into Amy allowing Maggie to gracefully glide through the door carrying two colorful carpetbags.

"Aunt Maggie, this is Amy. Amy, my Aunt Maggie."

"Very nice meeting you, Miss Maggie." Amy had to stop herself from curtsying.

Maggie lowered her glasses once again to give Amy a thorough looking over. "I know all about you. You're the young lady that's going to save the French Quarter from sinking below the Mississippi River."

"So I've heard."

"Spunky, aren't ya!"

"And a good game player, Aunt Maggie!" Danny added.

The boys took her bags and stayed close behind her skirt.

"She is, is she?" Maggie smiled and ruffled Danny's hair which made him almost swoon with joy.

Maggie plopped down in a huge Chippendale wing chair right in front of a roaring fire.

"Almost drowned, I did. Terrible weather outside."

Amy was intrigued. "Have you been here long? It's very noisy in the streets. I see you found your way through the tunnel."

"Aye, good thing the lads built this end of it. The streets are packed with people wearing very strange looking get ups. And to answer your question, me dear, I've been in town barely a few days. I flew right into the Irish Channel and visited Uncle Sean first until it was too noisy even for me." She had a big booming chuckle that moved even the air aside.

Jimmy smiled at his Aunt who sat in the wing chair like it was made just for her, with Danny, Liam and Paddy lounging adoringly at her feet.

"You were going somewhere, Jimmy?" Maggie looked over her glasses at him.

"Oh, yes. We're going to a Murder Mystery Dinner Party at a haunted plantation. I'll tell you all about it when we get back. Right now we have to go." Jimmy patted her hand.

"Sounds marvelous. I went to one years ago. Paris, yes, it was in Paris. Liam, take this to the kitchen. I'll have tea now."

Maggie opened one of her bags and pulled out a fitted case with a complete tea service. She had delicate cups and saucers with the tiniest blue flowers painted on them, a tea pot, sugar and creamer to match, and a tin of loose tea.

Amy wanted to ask Maggie about her experience at a Murder Mystery party but Jimmy was urging them on their way.

After saying their goodbyes they hurried along the tunnel. Amy counted the steps to the secret door that led into her bedroom. She looked to her left as she passed the familiar stone that, when pushed, opened the door. She guessed correctly.

They finally arrived at the door leading into the garden of The Golden Palace. Jimmy pushed a latch and they stepped into a storm outside.

Amy was used to storms with the very same intensity when she lived at the orphanage. She was pleased to see that the awnings had been rolled up and most of the light patio furniture had been stored away.

Someone had missed one umbrella, that had tipped over, taking a patio table with it. Tree limbs were strewn all about. Rain stung her cheeks, like needles. She followed Jimmy into the lobby of the hotel through a back door.

They must have looked a sorry sight, like two drenched tourists, but most of the other hotel guests didn't look much different. It was obvious they had all been caught in the storm and sought shelter in the hotel, guests or not.

Jimmy didn't pause for a second but hurried out the front door, with Amy behind him, to the waiting limo in front.

Their limo driver, Mickey Daly, had spent the morning driving two irritable tourists to an alligator swamp tour and back. The storm had put everyone in a terrible mood except for Mickey. He had a sunny disposition and a friendly word for everyone no matter how irritating they might be.

"Hi Mickey. Sorry we're going to get everything wet back here."

"Not a problem. The weather will improve."

Amy laughed. "I love positive thinking." Amy liked him immediately. She thanked him for waiting as she climbed into the limo with Jimmy crowding in behind her.

Mickey knew how valuable his passenger was. Before Marie had returned with Amy he had been making plans to leave the city, as was everyone. Now they were saved. Mickey was determined to make sure nothing happened to this charming young girl.

Mickey lowered the window between the front and the back.

"Miss Amy, I will be taking you to the Pirates Ball on Tuesday night. Everyone is thrilled. For many years we had only a parade but not the ball."

"Why is that?"

"We didn't have a queen, until now."

"I hope I'll be a good one. Was a pirate also one of your ancestors?"

"Indeed. Black Bart was my great, great, great...well a very way back grandfather of mine."

"I'll read all about him when I return to my Aunt's house. She has a wonderful library."

"Miss Amy, would you like to know a little about the French Quarter landmarks we are passing on our way to River Road?"

"Oh yes, please. I'm fascinated with everything about my new home."

Jimmy promptly fell into a light sleep which was annoying since she had planned on asking him about Aunt Maggie and the Irish Channel.

Mickey pointed out all the famous buildings and equally famous houses as they went past. Amy was especially interested in The magnificent St. Louis Cathedral right in front of Jackson Square. She wanted to know all about the statue in the middle of the park, too. Mickey was a font of knowledge. She pulled out a pad and a small pen from the pocket of her raincoat and started making notations about the places she wanted to visit.

"Jimmy, look at my list. Could we please visit all these places?"

Jimmy opened one eye, only to see what she was talking about. "Oh, my Gawd, you've turned into a tourist."

Amy laughed.

Mickey pushed the automatic button and the window between them slid up since they were now on River Road and wouldn't see anything exciting until they went past the plantations and they were well outside of town.

They traveled in silence for a while and then Mickey lowered the window between them. "Miss Any, would you like to see the Destrehan Plantation where they filmed part of a vampire movie—"

"You mean Interview With A Vampire?"

"That's the one."

"Yes! How fascinating!" Amy looked over at Jimmy who was once again snoring.

"They filmed the dining room scene there."

"With Brad Pitt and Tom Cruise. It was fantastic!"

"It's only twenty miles from New Orleans. It was built in 1787. And in 1830-1840 the architecture changed from French Colonial to Greek Revival."

Mickey drove past the plantation slowly while Amy imagined the scene with the French doors leading from the dining room wide open and the strong winds making the lace curtains whip in and out the doors.

She wished they had time to take the house tour that was advertised on a large sign and then walk around the grounds but it was getting late and the storm had led to detours and back roads that she was sure Mickey hadn't planned on taking.

They passed a few more magnificent plantations and Mickey promised that on the first sunny day he'd take her on a grand tour.

They stayed on River Road which was an appropriate name for a road that followed the Mississippi river, turning this way and that.

That passed towns that comprised of a main street, a café and a filling station. Soon Mickey turned at a sign that gave directions to St. Germaine.

She made a list of all the plantations they passed that she wanted to visit after this Pirates Ball was over. Destrehan was first on the list followed by the beautiful Oak Alley with two rows of oak trees flanking a path to the house with tree limbs that bowed, and met in the middle, sheltering a carriage driving to the front door. And Laura Plantation with the historical sharecropper cabins, and St. Joseph Plantation built in 1830, a still working sugar plantation, owned by the same family since 1877. And there was the Evergreen, the Houmas House, and the famous Rosedown."

"We're at Devereux Plantation." Jimmy was staring out the window.

There were ten gleaming white columns across the front with a wide veranda on the lower level and a spacious wrap around porch on the second and third floors. It gleamed pristine white in the late afternoon sun.

"Wow. It's beautiful...and very large."

"Did you see the for sale sign at the entrance to the drive?"

"Really? No, I didn't. What do you think they would ask for it?"

"Do you want to buy it? I could whip up that pot of gold we're so famous for."

"Are you serious?"

"NO!"

"Jimmy, stop that."

"Okay. Let's go."

Amy knocked on the separating window. "Mickey. Will you be waiting? I'm not sure how long the whole thing will take."

"I have some friends to visit. Jimmy knows how to contact me when you're ready to leave. Have fun. Don't let the ghosts get you."

Amy watched Mickey drive away before turning to Jimmy. "He was just kidding, right?"

"Sure." Jimmy turned with a grin and said "I heard these ghosts are not one bit evil...more like the friendly type, actually."

"Indeed! I'm on to you Jimmy O'Brien! So no more of your nonsense."

Jimmy followed behind Amy, grumbling all the way.

He couldn't see her big smile.

Annie swished her monkey tail and rested her chin on Serena's knee. "I wonder where Miss Amy is right now?"

Serena looked up from the Times Picayune she had been reading. "I know exactly where she is. Why aren't you out hanging by your new tail and scaring the squirrels in the courtyard?"

"Word is that she went to the Devereux Plantation for a Murder Mystery Dinner Party which sounds very exciting. I hear it's haunted, too."

"Why did you ask me if you knew?"

Annie gave her a big doggie smile.

"And where did you hear that?"

"The birds told me." Annie swished her tail.

"Well, the birds know. That's where she is. And now that you mentioned it I think I will give her a little gift that might come in very handy with all those ghosts around." Serena laughed.

"What is that, might I ask?"

"You know you should have been a hound dog with that nosy nose of yours."

Annie pouted.

"Oh, all right I'll tell you. It would be more fun if she could touch something and go back in time to see what happened. All she will have to do is wish to know. Maybe she'll see a ghost or two."

Annie, a ghost-loving dog, whirled around in joy.

Serena walked out to her crystal ball hovering above the fountain in the courtyard. She could see Amy and Jimmy O'Brien just arriving at the Plantation.

She waved her hands in the air and said,

"Touch something once, and if you wish it you'll see,
Past, present and what is to be."

Amy, with Jimmy still grumbling behind her, walked through massive twelve foot high double front doors into1830s plantation living.

A round mahogany antique table centered the front hall. Only the tour brochures covering the top of the table were modern.

A *Check In Here* sign pointed to the right.

A desk that held a computer, a printer, more brochures on the plantation, and a woman wearing a Gone With The Wind dress was sitting, peering over her glasses at them.

"Welcome. We love early guests. I'm Mary Devereux. You are Amy and Jimmy?"

"Indeed, we are." Jimmy answered cheerfully.

"Please sign our guest book. Unfortunately our Murder Mystery will be delayed for about an hour since the other guests are having trouble getting here."

"No problem." Amy looked around. "What a beautiful home."

"Thank you."

"I saw the For Sale sign. It must be hard to part with it."

"It is. This time of year is very festive with all the Mardi Gras parades. I'm so glad you decided to come to the Murder Mystery."

Amy picked up a pen to sign the guest book and she could hear Mary Devereux's thoughts clear as day...*too little income and too many repairs.*

"Maybe things will change."

"Maybe." Mary looked at Amy. It was almost as if the young girl could read her mind. Wanting to change the subject Mary quickly handed her a list of rooms. "You have first choice on the rooms for the Murder Mystery. You each choose where you want to start."

Amy took the list. The one that caught her eye immediately was the library.

"I want the library."

She passed the list to Jimmy.

"Good choice. I love the library, too." Mary handed her a large envelope. "Follow the instructions carefully."

Mary turned to Jimmy who was ready with his choice. "I'll take the Music Room right next door to Amy."

"Here is your packet." She handed him a similar envelope. "Due to the delay you might want to wander around the grounds. If you do then I would advise taking one of the umbrellas by the door. If not, you're welcome to have tea and coffee in the parlor across the hall until the other guests arrive."

"Thank you. I think we'll look around outside."

Jimmy took his time signing his name into the guest book. He loved looking at all the names of guests who stayed there before him.

In the meantime Amy picked up some brochures on the plantation, shoved them into the pocket of her jacket, along with her Murder Mystery instruction envelope, and walked over to the front door pulling a black umbrella from a large vase.

She waited until Jimmy had finished then walked out to the spacious veranda. Huge thunderclouds were starting to gather in the darkening sky.

"Let's go explore the cabins over there."

"Why don't I just sit here and you wander around." Jimmy stuffed his Murder Mystery instruction envelope into his pocket and climbed up on one of the many rocking chairs on the veranda.

He quickly hopped down when he saw Amy standing with her hands on her hips and a very determined look on her face.

"Follow me." Amy took off at a fast clip heading down a dirt road towards the row of hundred year old cabins that once held the workers on the plantation and now held only spider webs and roaches.

Amy could smell the rain in the air. It was fresh and scented with a riot of sweet jasmine, gardenias and pine trees. Living on the island she had been used to the smell of salt water and looking out at a view of either the ocean or dense forests. Here there was so much to see. She passed magnolia trees with flowers the size of saucers and she didn't know wild azaleas could grow so high in such profusion.

They arrived at the first of the cabins. Three wide planks served as stairs leading to a narrow porch with squeaky floorboards.

Jimmy sat down at the top of the stairs. "Do what you want. I'm not moving."

A screen door creaked on its hinges as a strong wind pushed it in and out. Dust drifted down as Amy grabbed the door and went in, shutting it behind her. She wished she could see what it was like during the days a sharecropper's family lived here. A strange feeling went through her hand. At once she was back in the 1800s. A woman was sitting on a stool, arms resting on a large farm table while she was peeling potatoes. She could hear the squeals of children rushing around doing chores while waiting for dinner to be cooked over the open fire.

These were places she had, until now, only read about. Seeing the real thing was so much better than reading about it. The scene faded out.

Amy called out. "Don't you want to come in?"

"Allergies."

"Oh, Jimmy." Amy sat next to him on the stairs. "It's exciting to see places I've only read about in books. You know I could actually see the family waiting for dinner to be cooked. They had a stew cooking in a pot over a roaring fire and the Mom was—"

"That library at St. Luke's must have been something."

"It was." Amy smiled. "I spent most of my day in that wonderful room. I remember whenever an encyclopedia salesman would brave the elements and make it to the island Mrs. Richardson would reward his efforts and buy the books he was selling. We had one whole bookcase dedicated to encyclopedia sets. Britannica was my favorite."

"You must have been very lonely."

"I was never lonely. The other kids at the orphanage were very young but I had my books. Whenever I was lonely I would pick out a new book to read and go into a world I'd never been in and visit places I would never have a chance to see."

They listened to the thunder growing louder.

"How long were you at the Orphanage?"

"I was left at the door of St. Luke's on Cutter's Island when I was five years old. The last memory I had was my birthday party with a big number five on a cake the night the ship went down. I try not to think of that because it was the last time I saw my mom and dad."

Amy clutched the apple green jade heart that lay brilliantly against her black sweater.

"That's a really beautiful heart, m'lady."

"Marie told me it belonged to my mother. She said my mom was wearing it the day she left home."

"I'd like to know how Jude and One Eye got it."

"Could we go back to Treasure Island and ask them?"

"Last I heard they were off the Island but they'll be at the Pirates Ball.

"When I hold it like this it grows warm. It's like she's right here beside me. I know she's alive somewhere."

"Did Marie tell you...I knew your mother. Marie brought me into the house one day and I met her. You look a lot like her." He said softly.

"Jimmy, I didn't know that. Then you know what this is all about. Tell me about the Pirates Ball. First I want to know all about this curse."

"How much time do we have?"

Amy checked her watch. "Forty minutes."

Jimmy nodded. "I'm going to tell you everything now. It started long ago. The Claiborne family had a beautiful young girl working as a kitchen maid. Her name was Serena."

"Serena!" Amy was thrilled. Was this the same Serena? She wanted to tell Jimmy about the love letter she had in her pocket, but he continued with his story.

"Yes. She was born in France. Her mother was a dancer in Paris but not making the money she thought she'd make she brought Serena to the French Quarter."

"What about her father?"

"He was a Romanian gypsy who left Paris before Serena was born."

"How did Serena end up working for the Claiborne family?"

"In the beginning her mother made a lot of money dancing but she started gambling it away and soon had nothing. Her mother died during a terrible epidemic that ravaged the city. When Serena was a young girl the Claiborne family took her in and apprenticed her to be a kitchen maid. She lived on the third floor with all the other help. She was very beautiful. Jean Lafitte came to the house on business one day and when he saw her..."

"You mean the pirate, Jean Lafitte?"

"Yes. He built an underground tunnel from the garden of his hotel to the Claiborne home where he could sneak in at night and bring Serena back to his hotel and woo her."

"How romantic."

"He planned to surprise her with a diamond ring and a marriage proposal but first he wanted to make one more trip to recover a large amount of treasure he had hidden in the Bayou. While he was gone, Governor Claiborne's wife found out about Serena's little trysts in the Claiborne house. You see the Governor's wife thought it unseemly that someone who worked in her house was carrying on like that so she threw Serena out with nothing."

"That was a very cruel thing to do."

"Serena couldn't find Lafitte and thought he had abandoned her. She left New Orleans that same night not knowing Lafitte was going to marry her. It was said she was going to have a child."

"What happened when he came back looking for her?"

"She had disappeared. No one knew where she had gone. He left in despair. It was rumored he died when his ship was sunk in the Caribbean."

"And Serena? What happened to her?"

"You've seen her...the Black Witch. You saw her the first day you arrived flying through the French Quarter on her carriage. Years later she returned to the French Quarter bringing with her a young son, Philippe. A son who is the image of his father...Jean Lafitte. They lived in peace for many years until one night, at a bar on Bourbon Street, Philippe got into a poker game with the Boudreaux Brothers, a group of Cajun shrimpers from the Bayou. They always won at cards because most of the time they cheated and got away with it. Everyone was scared of the Boudreaux boys but not Serena's son. He stood up to them and accused them of cheating. They beat him up and left him to die in Pirate's Alley."

"How awful."

"Your mother found him and secretly took care of him at the Claiborne mansion on Royal Street. Then they disappeared together. Your grandparents would never have approved of him since he had the bloodline of Jean Lafitte. Governor Claiborne hated Lafitte.

When Serena, the Black Witch, found out what had happened to her son she went into a rage. She cursed the Boudreaux brothers and turned them into Cajun rats, an animal with a man's face and a rat's body. They are around but rarely let themselves be seen. Then she cursed the Claiborne family for throwing her out like trash all those years ago."

"Jean Lafitte died in the 1800s. How could my father be his son? That would make him about---"

"---It's complicated."

"How complicated? And tell me about this curse."

"If a beautiful girl child, born a Claiborne, didn't reign as Queen before she turned nineteen then the French Quarter would sink below the Mississippi River."

"My Mom was supposed to reign as Queen, wasn't she?"

"Yes, but she ran off with Philippe. She was afraid if he stayed the Boudreaux boys would kill him. She didn't know that the Black Witch, with all her powers, was his Mother. Philippe was your father and that's why you could see the Black Witch the day you arrived in the French Quarter. No one else can. You're her granddaughter. And I'm sure she has had a hand in watching over you."

"Why is she going through with the curse?"

"I don't know. Ask Marie."

"I see now how important it was to bring me back to the French Quarter especially since the Ball is this coming Tuesday and I'm not yet nineteen."

"Yes. Marie was overjoyed when you were found."

A flash of lightning made Amy jump. "That was too close for comfort."

Ten seconds later it was followed by a loud ripping clap of thunder.

"That's it! Ten seconds means the storm is only two miles away. I suggest we get back to the main house."

"I agree. Jimmy, there is something I must show you." She started to retrieve the love letter in her pocket.

"I think it can wait. Was that a tornado over there?"

Looking up the clouds in the sky looked like black carbon paper being mashed about and tossed in the wind.

Amy quickly unfurled the house umbrella but worried it would do little to help Jimmy since he was so close to the ground. Amy tried to hurry him along.

"A little exercise wouldn't hurt. Do you play any sports?"

"I do indeed."

"What?"

"Little League." Jimmy roared with laughter.

She looked back but now Jimmy was wearing an Irish green rain slicker, rain boots and a little rain hat. She smiled. Another bit of Jimmy's magic.

But rain found a way inside his slicker so he complained all the way back to the house.

They ran through the front door just as the skies opened and the light rain turned into a torrential downpour. For now Amy had forgotten all about the love letter safe and unharmed.

Mary Devereux pointed to an open door across the hall.

"You'll find hot drinks and snacks in there. I'm still waiting for the rest of the guests to arrive."

An inviting log fire was blazing in the huge fireplace. A table against the wall held pots of hot tea, coffee and cocoa. Finger sandwiches filled a silver platter that matched the tea service.

"Jimmy?" She nodded towards the table.

"Tea, please, milk, two sugars."

She filled two mugs with tea. In her other hand she balanced a small plate with roast beef and chicken salad sandwiches fit for the Queen.

She placed the mugs, and the plate heaped with tiny sandwiches, on a tea table between two wing chairs facing the warm fire. Pulling out her envelope she began to read her instructions for the Murder Mystery Game.

Not looking up from her instructions she said "Jimmy, I suggest you do the same and leave some of the roast beef for me."

He gave her a guilty look as right that minute he was finishing the last of the roast beef finger sandwiches.

There were two pages of directions. The first page had big capital letters that said **SHARE THIS INFORMATION WITH EVERYONE.** You are a librarian from New Orleans doing research. You came here because you are interested in the unique history of plantation life in the 1800s at Devereux.

The second page said **DO NOT SHARE THIS INFORMATION WITH ANYONE. FOR YOUR CHARACTER ONLY.** You are really here to locate a map, hidden somewhere in the library, that will reveal the location of Jean Lafitte's treasure chest. There is only one person here who wants to buy the plantation. If you eliminate the competition you can buy the plantation yourself and take your time finding the treasure chest.

That certainly is a motivation for murder, Amy thought. Putting the pages back in the envelope she returned it to her pocket.

Jimmy read his pages and was making quick work of the chicken salad finger sandwiches when Amy interrupted him just as he was taking a final bite.

"Jimmy...what do your instructions say?"

At that moment the lights went out.

Amy, Queen of the Pirates Ball

CHAPTER EIGHT
Amy Meets Her Grandmother, The Black Witch

Kathy Dubois patted the dashboard of her 1965 Ford Mustang, "We made it." When she started nursing school her Dad had given her the restored convertible and said "Take good care of the old girl." And she did.

She took notice of the For Sale sign attached to a brick column beside the open wrought iron gates to Devereux Plantation.

She was going to her first Murder Mystery Dinner Party at a haunted bed & breakfast. She wondered if there were other guests coming because of the For Sale sign.

Strong winds made her car shift on the gravel driveway and the driving rain made it very hard to see anything at all. Thunder and a close bolt of lightning made the ground shake.

A strange noise came from under the hood and then nothing. Her car was dead as a doornail.

No matter how many times she tried to turn it over...nothing. It wasn't gas. She had stopped in the last town back and filled up before the storm hit.

A car pulled up next to her.

The hum of a power window going down and the loud sound of the rain hitting the hood of her car blocked out the sounds of the struggle Kathy was making to get her window down.

"Can I help?"

Now that she had a better view she realized a huge SUV, big enough to cast a shadow, hovered, shaking with RPM energy.

Kathy recognized the driver immediately. He was Billy Bolt Butler, the newest Quarterback of the New Orleans Saints football team. He was very handsome and had a car that worked!

"My car broke down." That had to rank up there with all time stupid responses. She stared straight ahead in embarrassment.

"Get in. I'm going to Devereux."

Another car had pulled up and was waiting patiently as the two cars blocked the drivable part of the crushed shell driveway.

Kathy jumped out of her car and into Billy's.

"Thanks."

Billy pulled in front of Kathy's Mustang and the waiting car roared past them. A *Just Married* sign in the back window said it all.

Billy followed them at a slower speed. "Wow! They're going to wear out soon."

They both laughed.

"I'm Billy."

"Kathy. Thank you for the lift."

"Interested in buying Devereux?"

Kathy smiled. In her dreams maybe. "I'm Just here for the Murder Mystery Dinner Party."

"I signed up, too. I've never been to one."

"They're fun. I went to one a year ago at a B&B in New Orleans."

"You're from New Orleans?"

"Born and raised."

"So am I."

Who didn't know that, Kathy thought, since it was in all the media releases?

At that moment all the lights in the big house blinked off and then on again.

"Did you see that?"

"That's certainly possible with a storm like this."

They pulled up in front of Devereux and parked on the crushed shell driveway behind the newlywed speed demons. Billy rushed around to open her door. With a hand under her arm Billy maneuvered her like he was running down the field with the ball.

Seamus was in awe at the beauty of the plantation as Angus stopped at the entrance gates leading down the gravel road to the front of Devereux.

"Drop me off here, Angus. I'll give ye a call when it's over and meet ye right here, okay?"

"Don't ye want me to drop ye off in

front?" "No, thanks."

"I hope ye made a reservation for the night because ye might be staying. I'm not sure about this weather. These rural areas flood mighty fast."

"I made a reservation just in case. I'll call ye."

Kathy and Billy were cold and damp when they got inside. Their rain gear joined the others on hooks by the front door. A huge log fire in the hall was warm and welcoming.

The hostess was talking to Marsha and Mark Houston, the honeymoon couple. Billy and Kathy stood behind them. Mary Devereux told them the same information she'd told Amy and Jimmy about reading the contents of the envelope and having hot drinks and snacks in the parlor across the hall.

Marsha and Mark picked The Dining Room and Kitchen.

Billy chose The TV Room and Kathy was very happy with the Conservatory.

Mary explained that the last two guests would not be coming because of the storm so she and her brother Tom would take the double parlors, one on each side of the grand hallway.

Usually there were eight guests in the eight downstairs rooms. But it would certainly work with only six guests, too. Mary and her sister, Delia, wrote the Murder Mysteries for any contingencies. Mary always played the dead body. Delia, the excellent chef in the family cooked dinner for all the guests. This was truly a family business.

Suggesting her guests join Amy and Jimmy in the parlor, she picked up a walkie talkie and called her brother Tom. She asked him to bring a basket of flashlights at once and to tell her sister there would be two less for dinner tonight.

Mary waited for him to arrive, giving her newest guests time to read their Murder Mystery instructions.

Marsha and Mark bypassed the tea table and went right to reading the contents of their envelopes. They had the same directions. They were to tell everyone they were at Devereux because their hotel was over-booked from now until after Mardi Gras. Having never been to Mardi Gras they had no idea it would be so crowded so they didn't confirm their reservations ahead of time as they had been advised to do. The secret information was that they were really undercover reporters for a Paranormal Website. If they reported that Devereux was no more haunted than the St. Louis Cathedral in the French Quarter then it meant they would have the lead story online and perhaps cancel the sale of the plantation as a haunted B&B.

Mark briefly wondered if his character might be the villain because they were here under false pretenses. Would writing a bad review have him fighting for his life?

Billy Bolt Butler's story was that he had been teased about his fear of ghosts. Some of his Saints teammates bet him he would chicken out and not even show up.

The secret information was that he loved a good ghost story and was really here to look over the B&B and maybe make an offer on the place. His financial advisor, Joe Jennings, told him it would be a good investment. A Geologist friend told him there was an undiscovered source of oil on the property. He knew someone else was also here to make a serious offer on buying Devereux. Of course if that person had an unfortunate accident then nothing would stand in his way. He thought for sure he would be the villain because oil meant money and some people would do anything for money!

Kathy was to tell everyone was that she was in nursing school which just happened to be true.

Her secret information was that she was here to buy Devereux and nothing was going to stand in her way. In

1898 her great, great grandfather had won Devereux in a very private poker game on the Mississippi Queen Riverboat. Then Charles Devereux had reneged on the deal and had her grandfather tossed into jail on a trumped up charge. When he was finally released from jail, Devereux went back to his plantation surrounded by newly hired guards. She wanted revenge. She loved her secret story. This was going to be a night to remember.

Kathy wondered if her character would be the villain since after all revenge is a common motive for murder.

Tom stood at the door to the parlor holding the basket of flashlights. Mary decided she had given her guests enough time to get ready so she crossed the hall, opened the parlor door and they went inside.

"Good evening, everyone. First, I want to introduce my brother, Tom. Our electricity went off, and thankfully back on again but I expect with this storm it may happen again and it might be longer next time so Tom will be passing out flashlights to everyone, just in case."

"Does the game stop if the lights go off?" Mark asked.

"If the lights go out use your flashlights and keep going with the game. The electric company usually gets things back on line quickly so we shouldn't be inconvenienced for very long."

"Does the Mississippi River ever flood the area?" Billy asked.

"We're a half mile to the River. I've never had to retreat to the third floor in any of the hurricanes. The roads might flood, which happens in a big storm but don't worry. Devereux has ten bedrooms on the second floor and six on the third floor. You are all welcome to stay, free of charge, until the roads are passable. And all of our kitchen appliances are run on propane for just such an emergency, so we will not go hungry."

Tom gave out all his flashlights.

Everyone in the room seemed relieved at this information.

Marsha Houston spoke first. "Thank you for your hospitality. The brochure said Devereux was once the site of the town City Hall."

"Yes. Actually Devereux was the entire town. The downstairs of the plantation, where we are now, was used for many purposes. One room held all the records for City Hall. You could come here and transact business. Another room was the Post Office. There was a Dry Goods Store, a Pharmacy, a butcher shop, cheese store and bakery.

It was probably too dark to see when you arrived but there's a road that runs down the side of the house to the Mississippi River. Plantation owners from miles around brought their goods to be loaded onto ships tied up at the Devereux dock, which is still standing.

There's also a chapel on the grounds, now just a ruin, but in the 1800's every Sunday morning there was Mass for anyone who wanted to go. You could get baptized and married there and they even had occasional funeral services. The deceased were buried in a cemetery about five miles from here. Devereux family members are buried in a special cemetery in the woods near the house."

"Wow." Billy looked around the room. "I had no idea about the importance of Devereux Plantation in this area."

Kathy spoke up. "I heard the plantation was lost in a poker game in 1898."

"Just a bedtime story. It's irrational to think a Devereux would be so careless to lose an entire plantation over a silly game." Mary smiled.

"But it was in the newspaper—" Kathy insisted not knowing if it was or not.

"A lot of things are in the newspaper. At the end of the Murder Mystery my sister, Delia, a world class chef, has planned a wonderful dinner for us but first we'll go over the rules for the game."

"This is going to be such fun." Amy whispered to Jimmy who looked like he was more interested in eating than playing.

"You start out by going to the room you chose. The rooms you chose are all on this floor. There are no stairs to climb. Each room has a table with a piece of paper giving you a clue. What you find will lead you to go on but you cannot leave your first room until you hear the bell chime over the door. That only applies to the first room. Does everyone understand what to do?"

There were nods of enthusiastic agreement all around.

"And whoever finds the murder victim call out, loudly, at once."

A buzz of excitement meant this would be a successful Murder Mystery. She could sure use the publicity. Having to sell Devereux was a reality unless she miraculously found the money to effect the needed repairs to keep the place from collapsing around her.

Amy and Jimmy were the first out the door. The library, with the music room next door, were the first rooms beyond the parlor. They parted and went in search of their first clue.

The library was not large but very elegant. The carved wood bookcases were a color of rich butter. The walls were painted Oriental Jade. Heavy ornate molding, in the same color wood as the bookcases, was made into ornate turned columns running from the bottom to the top of each six foot section of books. Amy's glance went immediately to the table in the middle of the room. A small sealed envelope rested on top.

She could hear someone playing the piano next door. She didn't know Jimmy could play or maybe it was one of those player pianos.

Spying a strange bit of exercise equipment in the corner Jimmy abandoned the piano and went over to see what the new equipment was all about. He slipped his feet into straps and lying back on a long board he pushed off, turning upside down.

He had an attack of the giggles. Everything was upside down. Even Amy was—Amy?

Amy entered the music room from a small door in the middle of the bookcases.

Bending upside down to talk to him she asked, "What are you doing?"

"Hanging upside down. What does it look like?"

"It looks like a Mediaeval Torture Device."

"Well, it's not! It's absolutely wonderful for the back. You should try it sometime."

Amy laughed and straightened up. "Did you find your next clue?"

"I did, thank you. You better hurry and find yours before the bell rings."

"See you later." Amy left the way she had come, shutting the door behind her.

Jimmy realized what a predicament he was in since he was too short to have the momentum to right himself. Grumbling he reached into his pocket and tossed some gold dust into the air and magically the board righted itself. Jimmy scrambled out of the foot straps and went in search of his clue.

Tearing open the envelope from the table Amy read, "Your next clue is in a book titled, _Jean Lafitte's Hidden Treasure._ You can find the book on the top shelf....

A library ladder was conveniently placed at the bookcase that ended at huge French doors.

Seamus approached Devereux Plantation cautiously. He was glad Angus had not made a big deal about dropping him off at the entrance gate. He didn't want to have to explain why he hugged the shadows and didn't go inside the house like a regular guest.

He looked in all the windows. Amy had to be in one of the rooms.

When he got to the library he was in luck. She had just entered the room...alone. He stood outside two huge multi-paned beveled glass doors. Heavy brocade drapes with tie backs on each side allowed him to see inside.

Seamus waited patiently in the raging storm. A sudden tug on his leg and Bubba, wearing a miner's light on a tiny little baseball cap, scrambled up his leg and perched on his shoulder.

"Hey, Cher, comme ce va?"

"Be quiet! What are ye doing here? Never mind...be quiet!"

"She can't hear us out here. With these thick walls she wouldn't hear a tornado if it went by." Bubba sneered.

"Why are ye wearing that stupid light on ye're head?"

"If you must know I'm kind of close to the ground and I don't want to fall into a hole. Any more questions?"

"I don't want anything to happen to her. I changed me mind. I'm going back to me ferryboat. Anyway, it's not her fault if she remembers. By the way, how did ye get here? It's a long way from the city."

"My family...shrimp boats...remember? They're waiting for me at the dock. Now please answer my question. You said it's not her fault if she remembers...what?"

"Keep quiet!"

Changing the plan was the stupid Irish guy's decision but Bubba hadn't changed his mind. He still had his reasons but now he kept them to himself.

At that moment the lights went out in the entire house again.

"Darn!" Taken by surprise by the lights going out Bubba leaned forward. Trying to keep his balance his little rat paws flailed wildly. The light on his little baseball cap hit the delicate glass in the french door.

When the lights went out Amy had just found the book with her next clue. Clicking on her flashlight, she started down the ladder.

The sound of something hitting glass caught her attention. She aimed her flashlight at the french doors hoping the house lights would go back on.

Everything happened at once. The lights came back on and Amy's flashlight highlighted the scene outside the doors. She stared with horror at Bubba, a rat with a man's face, perched on Seamus' shoulder while Seamus was staring at her with a terrified look on his face. They all screamed at once.

Amy backed away from the french doors so fast she tripped on the book she had dropped. She landed on the hard wood floor.

Mary Devereux was lying down on the floor of the parlor waiting to be discovered. She loved being the "body" at the Murder Mystery parties since it was so easy to just lie there. The lights went out but she prayed they would go back on and they did. She had just gotten comfortable again when she heard Amy scream.

What now, she thought, as she scrambled to her feet.

The honeymoon couple had just discovered more little finger sandwiches in the kitchen refrigerator and were helping themselves when they heard the scream.

Kathy and Billy bumped into each other outside their rooms. They weren't sure exactly where the scream came from.

They all converged into the hallway.

Jimmy had been the first one into the library and seeing Amy laying on the floor thought she was the Murder Mystery dead body so he was running around, yelling "I'm first! I found the body! I'm first!"

Mary Devereux, and all the rest of the guests that had piled up behind her, spilled through the library door.

Mary spoke first. "Oh, no! I'm supposed to be the dead body in the parlor. What happened to Amy?"

Amy had been lying there, with her eyes closed, hoping when she opened them that horrid little rat person, sitting on Seamus' shoulder, would be gone. Seamus? She was right all along. He had been following her.

Jimmy ran to Amy side wringing his hands in a frantic manner. "Please be okay. What will I tell Marie? She'll kill me or turn me into a lawn fixture...I'm not sure which is worse."

Kathy gasped.

Jimmy realized what he said was a bit strange for this crowd. "Amy, Amy, say you're okay."

Amy opened her eyes. "I'm fine. Bit of a headache though."

"Thank goodness you can talk." Jimmy was so relieved he wanted to cry.

"We need an ambulance." Mary was frantic.

Kathy stepped forward. "I'm in Nursing School in Metairie. I don't think you're going to get anybody out here tonight. I'll check on Amy."

"Thank you, thank you!" Mary stood there wringing her hands.

Amy sat up. "Jimmy, there's that place again...Metairie!"

Jimmy stopped hopping around and ran across the room yelling "I have to call Marie! I have to call Marie! I'll be right back."

Amy turned her attention to Kathy. "Tell me, do you say Gawd and Dawlin'?"

Kathy smiled. "Some people do. I don't. I'm from Uptown."

"New Orleans is a very confusing place. There's Metairie, now I find out there's a place called Uptown, Mid

City, of course the French Quarter, in and out, the Lakefront, the Garden District...have I left out anything?"

"There are a few more but that's close enough."

"And it's so strange...people keep asking me where I went to High School. Where did you go?"

"Dominican...an all girl Catholic school. It's in Uptown. Where are you from, Amy?"

"I grew up on a small island in the Irish Sea." "No wonder you're so confused." "No wonder."

Amy noticed Mary looked at Kathy when she mentioned Dominican.

Mary clicked off her walkie talkie. "Kathy, my sister Delia and I both went to Dominican."

"Oh, what year?"

"Delia is a year older than me and graduated first. I was in the last graduating class on St. Charles."

"Oh! I loved that campus!"

"We did, too."

Amy put Dominican on her list of places to visit. "Amazing. Doesn't anyone ask where you went to college?"

Mary smiled.

Kathy spoke to Mary. "She's okay."

Jimmy listened to the exchange with Kathy, relieved Amy was not hurt.

Marie didn't answer the phone. He decided to call Paddy and send him over to find Marie and explain where they were and why Amy didn't come back from playing The Pirate Treasure Game at his house. For the time being he would escape Marie's wrath. She was definitely going to be furious over his taking Amy out of the French Quarter.

Danny answered on the second ring.

"Hi, Jimmy. Uh, oh..."

Marie took the phone away and spoke through gritted teeth, "Well, hello, Jimmy. I'm having a nice visit with Aunt Maggie and the boys."

"What a surprise, isn't it? He put on a very pretend jolly voice. "Didn't expect Maggie until Christmas! Anyway I'm with Amy and we're at this really fun—"

"I <u>know</u> where you are." Cutting him off in mid sentence Marie hissed into the phone, making Jimmy shiver with dread at what was to come. "Danny told me. We'll have a nice long talk about this when you get back. Right now stay where you are. I'll pick you up tomorrow."

"Okay, Dokey." Jimmy trilled lightly. He was frantic but couldn't let anyone in the room know.

"Stop that!" Marie took a moment to calm herself. She snarled into the phone. "You're in big trouble with me, buddy. You were NOT to take Amy anywhere but your house. The roads are flooded otherwise I'd come there right this minute and drag your little Leprechaun self back here. Do we understand each other?"

Jimmy said loudly so everyone could hear. "Oh that's so wonderful. Amy sends a big hello. Thank you so very much. See you tomorrow."

He quickly hung up the phone and called Mickey Daly, their driver, but he already guessed that Mickey was well out of the flooded roads and back in New Orleans by now.

"Sorry, Jimmy. My boss called me back to the city before the roads were washed out..."

"I figured as much. Marie's coming for us in the morning." Jimmy tried not to sound like depression warmed over.

"That works out well." Mickey tried to stay upbeat and positive.

"You think so, huh?" Jimmy wanted to kick something.

Jimmy prayed that by tomorrow Marie might have mellowed out and not turn him into a lawn statue but he didn't plan on anything good happening. Well there was one thing...she had to wait until after Mardi Gras since she was relying on him to get Amy to the Ball on time.

"Mistress, Mistress!" Annie came running in from the courtyard shaking rain water off her back.

Serena put the "Gone With The Wind" DVD she was watching on hold and looked at the wet dog.

"What!"

"I was just hanging out in the oak tree and I happened to glance at the crystal ball and Miss Amy is lying on the floor in a strange house...with her eyes closed."

Serena literally flew to the crystal ball in the courtyard. She stood in the pouring rain to see her precious granddaughter now sitting up with everyone around her looking panicked.

"Get the carriage out." She shouted.

Annie raced to the barn behind the house and told Perkins, their driver, to get the horses and the carriage to the porte cochere fast. The Mistress was going somewhere. And she probably needed him to drive, too.

Perkins had never seen Annie in such a state so the carriage was ready to go in minutes.

"Well, get in!" Serena looked at Annie who was wide eyed with anticipation at being part of this adventure.

Annie leaped into the carriage. "Thank you! Thank you. This is the first time you've taken me with you since I had that little accident that we won't speak of since I was really, really sorry and—"

"—Stop talking! And don't make me wish it's the last and keep that monkey tail out of sight."

"Devereux Plantation!" Serena shouted to Perkins.

Annie grinned and curled up next to the large carriage window, resting her chin on the ledge she watched the city disappear below them. She quickly fell asleep.

They flew about a thousand feet up following the Mississippi River.

Seamus was hiding in the trees surrounding the plantation. The last he saw of Bubba was the rat jumping on the back of a motor scooter and was headed down a gravel road on the side of the house that led to the Mississippi River. Bubba told him that he had arrived on one of the Boudreaux fishing boats. He guessed he was going back the way he had come.

Bubba clung to his cousin's broad shoulders.

"Beau Boy, you were right. That Irish guy, Seamus, messed it up for us again. Next time we do it without him. Next time we get it right. I'll tell you my plan when we get on the boat."

The scooter made it down the rutted dirt road ending at a decrepit dock where a large fishing trawler was tied up.

Beau pushed his scooter down the dock, over the gangplank and onto the deck of the boat where he tied it down securely. Bubba clung to his shoulder.

They cast off and were safely under way before Bubba spoke his thoughts.

"We're gonna kidnap that girl and hold her hostage.

As long as we have her we're safe. That old Witch, Serena, wouldn't dare do us any harm or it'll be au revoir to her precious. Hey, we can't depend on that Irish guy. He's out of it. Said he was goin' back to where he comes from. I knew from the start not to trust him but now he'll be out of our way."

"I don't know, Bubba. I sure don't want to get turned into a rat thing like you." Bubba chose to ignore the comment. "Listen, if we have the girl, I can force the witch to change me and my brothers back to our human selves or the girl will suffer. Believe me, cher, when she hears that then the old hag will change her tune fast enough, you'll see. Mess with the Boudreaux Brothers and it's bye-bye Amy."

"You can't mean that, Bubba. If you do away with the girl the witch will come after all of us for sure."

Bubba smacked his cousin's ear with one paw. "What are you...stupid or somethin'? It won't get that far. We just threaten to do her harm. Do ya understand now?"

"Oh, yeah! I get it, Bubba! You're really smart. I didn't think of that."

Bubba wiggled his tail. He was the smartest of the bunch, he knew that for sure.

Seamus called Angus on his cell phone. "I imagine ye're not coming back this way tonight?"

"Ye guessed right. Roads are closed. I'm staying with me friends. Things will be better in the morning. Ye have a reservation there for the night, don't ye?"

"I do." *But I'd rather be making reservations to return to Ireland,* he thought. Unfortunately, with all the roads flooded the other guests, including Amy, would not be leaving, which presented a problem. He would have to throw up a shelter in the dense forest surrounding the house. It wouldn't be the first time he was caught out in the rain.

He started to go back and retrieve his cap, hoping it was still on the ground. But he would have to wait. All the lights were on inside and out. Rain pounded on his head and trickled down his back. He was cold, hungry and now getting very wet. He didn't want to run into Amy and have to explain what he was doing there so he waited for everyone to retire for the night. Later he'd knock on the door explaining that he had been caught in the storm. Luckily he had made a room reservation for the night.

When Jimmy got off the phone, Amy was sitting in an overstuffed chair and the room was empty. "Where did everyone go?" He asked.

"They are continuing with the game. I asked for time to rest here. Listen, Jimmy, I saw the ferryboat guy again. He was outside the doors. An awful looking rat person was on his shoulder and knocked his hat off his head. Go see if you can find it outside. It's a black fisherman's cap."

Jimmy hurried to the door, hoping the wind hadn't blown it away, hoping it was not just Amy's imagination.

Much to his surprise the wind and rain had plastered a black cap against the side of the house. He snatched it up, looked around, and then rushed back inside making sure he locked the door behind him.

Amy shuttered. "I told you I was being followed and who was that horrible rat person? I've never seen anything like that."

"I believe you now about that ferry boat guy. The rat person I imagine is one of the Boudreaux brothers. Remember I told you about them back at the cabin. They were the ones who cheated in poker. The Black Witch changed them into rat people for beating up her son.

"Jimmy, would you get me a cup of tea." "Sure."

He reluctantly left her alone in the room.

Amy held the cap tightly and wished she could see everything that had happened since she was rescued by Seamus in the Irish Sea that horrible night.

A fishing boat slowly appeared out of a dense fog. A man she knew as Seamus was standing on the stern searching for someone. He frantically swung a huge boat light over the water in all directions. The only sounds were the metal groan of the light followed by the creaking of the wood hull of the fishing boat. And always the howl of the wind, the brilliant flash of lightning and crash of thunder.

Seamus saw something that made him jump with joy. He quickly maneuvered close to an overturned lifeboat where a very young girl, who looked like she was sleeping, was supported on top of the boat by someone in the water.

"First the girl!" The man in the water pushed her into the hands of the fisherman who dropped her on top of a pile of blankets.

He quickly turned his attention to the man in the water and with one huge pull lifted him into the boat.

They embraced with joy.

She lay still with her eyes closed, but not sleeping, and heard bits of conversation tossed to her by fierce winds around them.

"I was afraid...the Captain...bad...sank the ship...insurance money...will kill me and all..."

"He will never know ye survived. I will hide ye." "What about the girl?"

"Poor thing. She's passed out...tell me...her parents..."

"I donna know...I only know her name is Amy. I assume...she and I...alone...lucky."

"I'll take her to....then ye disappear...live far away...can't tell...not even Mama."

"Seamus, take care...of Mama."

"Mama...yes...no worry. I'll take care..."

"So sorry..."

"Not your fault. Never trusted Captain Murphy....bad man."

The boat started to disappear into the quickly returning fog bank.

Amy looked around realizing she was back at the plantation.

Now she wished to know what Seamus had said tonight outside the window.

It was raining hard. That awful rat was on his shoulder. They were watching her. She heard Seamus say he didn't want any harm coming to her. It wasn't her fault that she couldn't remember that night.

Seamus said he changed his mind. All he wants is to go back home. Then the rat jumped off Seamus' shoulder and scrambled onto the shoulder of someone driving a motor scooter. They were headed for the River.

Before more could be revealed to her Jimmy came back into the room carrying two mugs of steaming tea.

Amy leaped up, crossed the room, opened the doors and dropped the hat on the ground. If he was still around he could have his hat back. Come to think of it she had never seen him without it.

As Serena's carriage flew over the plantation she looked down and saw a large shrimp boat pulling away from the Devereux dock.

She smiled. She had something very special in mind for that Cajun rat and the rest of his brothers, yes something very special and very horrible.

Tapping the window. "Perkins. The front gate."

The carriage landed gently on the road and in an instant turned into an ancient old Rolls, mud splattered and covered with leaves and twigs. Just the sort of car that would have gone through a storm to get there.

Serena turned herself into an image of Marie and her driver, Perkins into Marcel, Marie's husband.

Having worked for the Mistress for over a hundred years nothing came as a surprise to the elderly driver. He drove down the long drive to the front door of Devereux.

The doorbell chimed. Having a Bed & Breakfast meant guests went in and out at will. *Who would be outside in this weather?* Mary wondered. It took Mary by surprise when the woman at the door said she was Marie and was there to take Amy home. The woman explained that they had taken still open back roads and they had to hurry before even those were closing.

"Thank you for coming out on such a horrible night. Amy and Jimmy were welcome to spend the night here."

"Her Aunt Lily wants Amy home tonight."

"Please come this way. I think she was expecting you tomorrow morning. She's in the Library."

"You have a lovely plantation. I see it's for sale."

I wish it wasn't, Mary thought with a sigh.

"Amy...Amy...Marie is here to take you home."

Amy, in her thoughts was still back at the Devereux dock and the rat person, was momentarily confused.

Jimmy knew the minute Mary walked into the room followed by someone calling herself Marie that it definitely was not Marie. Only Serena could turn herself into such a perfect copy.

Actually he was relieved Serena was here because he had known for ages that she was Amy's grandmother and if there was only one person who could take care of Amy better than he could and that was Serena.

Before Marie came into the room Amy had told Jimmy that Seamus only wanted to go back home and meant her no harm but the rat person was making plans to kidnap her.

Jimmy was sure the real Marie was so angry about his taking Amy out of the city the minute they got back she would turn him onto a horrible concrete gnome for someone's front yard.

He knew for a fact that all those yard gnomes you see are Leprechauns who ran into bad luck. And once turned into a concrete gnome there is no going back.

And now if he displeased Serena...well...he wondered if there were any Leprechaun rats? He sure hoped not. Cajuns and Irish don't mix very well. Jimmy shivered at the thought.

Jimmy heard Serena's voice in his head telling him she was not going to turn him into anything. She said that he'd done a good job taking care of her precious granddaughter and nobody was going to turn him into anything.

What a relief! Jimmy thought exhaling loudly. Amy gave him a strange look wondering why he'd been holding his breath. "Well hello there, Marie. Thought you weren't coming until the morning. Ha, ha, ha. Well, there it is. We've had a wonderful time and the best finger sandwiches and—"

Serena narrowed her eyes at him. "Shut up before I change my mind!"

Jimmy withered under her brief glance. She certainly sounded like Marie.

Serena turned to Mary. "Thank you for taking care of Amy...and her friend."

Amy thought that was strange. Marie and Jimmy were cousins but now was not the best time to talk about family connections. "How did you get here so fast?"

Jimmy spoke quickly hoping to divert Amy's attention. "Amy, we're on our way back home. Isn't that wonderful? Let's thank Mary and not keep Marie waiting."

"Good idea." Serena gave him a smile that said he was getting better.

Amy handed the book about Jean Lafitte to Mary. "Thank you. Please tell everyone goodbye for us."

"I will. You and Jimmy have a free invitation any time you want to return for a Murder Mystery. You, too, Marie."

That's highly unlikely, Jimmy thought, as he practically pushed Amy out the door, while thanking Mary profusely.

"Wow! I didn't know Aunt Lily had <u>this</u> in the garage." She was talking about the Rolls waiting in front with the engine idling.

Jimmy hurried her inside. "Wait until you see the seats...I bet it's all leather."

Annie was still sleeping with her tail curled up under her.

"What a surprise Marie. I didn't know you had a dog."

Jimmy gasped. "I have a feeling there are much bigger surprises in store, Amy. So scoot over."

The minute Serena got in the car the driver started driving slowly back to the road outside the gates.

"Did you see the For Sale sign? Why do you think the plantation is for sale?" Amy wondered while looking at the sign.

Jimmy had asked Mary that same question. "She told me she had more repairs that she had money to fix them. The plantation has been in the family for over 200 years."

"Oh, I'm so sorry. I liked her. She was very kind to us." Amy looked sad.

Serena, with a snap of her fingers and a twist of her wrist she made sure every repair on the plantation would be completed before Mary woke up in the morning. It was the least she could do for the kindness she had shown to her beloved granddaughter

Before they got to the road outside the entrance gates Jimmy was fast asleep.

"Poor thing. He's been on his feet since early this morning. On the way over here he fell asleep the minute he got in the car, too."

"We won't wake him." Serena smiled. It had more to do with the sleep powder that she sent his way than exhaustion.

The car came to a stop.

"I have something to tell you. I'm Serena, I'm your Grandmother. Philippe was my son. I have so much to tell you but first we have to get home. In a few seconds this car will turn into my carriage. And I will turn into....oh, never mind. Hold on."

Serena said "Perkins" and instantly the entire car faded and they were sitting in the back of a black carriage pulled by four magnificent black horses with plumes, and they were flying through the air.

"You're the Black Witch and my Grandmother!"

"That's why you could see me when you drove home from the airport but please stop saying 'Black Witch.' I never did like that name so Grandmother or Granny will do just fine."

Laughing with joy she covered her Grandmother's hand with hers.

Serena! Was this the Serena in her letter?

"I have something to show you. It's addressed to you. I found this in my Mother's bedroom in Aunt Lily's house."

Amy carefully pulled out the love note and handed it to Serena.

She watched as Serena read the letter. Tears ran down Serena's cheeks.

She turned to her Granddaughter. "You can't know how happy this makes me. Thank you!" She folded the note and pressed it to her heart. When she left the Claiborne house many centuries ago she was alone in the world. It comforted her at the time to cast a spell making Lafitte immortal and keeping him safe. Now she knew by his own words that he loved her. She would make a spell to bring him to her.

CHAPTER NINE
Seamus Changes His Mind

Seamus watched Amy and her friends get into the big car. He briefly wondered how they got though the flooded roads to get here and how they were going to get back but right now he was more concerned with getting inside for food and shelter. It was a terrible night for being outside he thought as he watched them drive away.

Trudging across the lawn he thought about the little guy with Amy. He had seen her with the same person before but he had been concentrating only on Amy and hadn't really paid any attention to her friend. He was paying attention now. It was probably his imagination but the little guy looked like...a Leprechaun!*How ridiculous is that?* He thought, laughing out loud.

Dodging heavy rain he made his way to the front door of the plantation and rang the doorbell.

Mary opened the door to see a man drenched to the bone standing there, shivering.

"I have a reservation for

tonight." "Come in, come in."

Amy looked out the carriage window at the Mississippi River below them. Tears came to her eyes.

"Do you know where my mother and father

are?" "Do you remember what happened?"

"I remember a loud noise and flashing red lights then people crying. The ship was sinking. They put me in a boat with other children. I don't remember anything else. I was saved by someone who brought me to an orphanage on an island. I've been there for the past thirteen years. I slowly started remembering things. I never forgot my mother but I was told all the Americans had died at sea. I didn't believe that. I could sense my mother around me all the time, but not my father. Please tell me."

"He saved your mother. They were in a lifeboat. They saw a mother and two children clutching a piece of wood in the water. Your father gave up his place in the boat for them. A wave took him away." Serena knew she had made her son immortal when he left with Celeste. She knew it was his choice to return.

"Oh, Papa." Amy looked out at the Mississippi River below them. "I knew in my heart he would have come for me if he could. And my mother?"

"You have only to ask the jade heart for the answer."

Amy clutched the heart that hung around her neck on a strong titanium chain and wished to see where her mother was. She fell into a sleep like trance.

She was in a dark room. There was a small cot where the slight figure of a woman was sleeping.

"Mama" she called.

Reluctantly Celeste sat up and looked around. She had this same dream so many times but tonight was different. Someone she knew was there in the mist of her memories. It was a young woman. She knew it was her daughter as any mother knows her own child.

"Oh Mama, I have missed you for so long. I was rescued that night and taken to an orphanage. Aunt Lily found me and brought me home to the French Quarter."

Celeste cried out, trying to see her in the dark. "Come sit by me. Is it really you? Every night I prayed for you. They told me all the children died. I saw the overturned lifeboat."

"You used to call me your brave little girl." "Your father? Do you know?"

"I don't think he survived. Grandmother Serena told me how he gave his seat to a mother and her children and then a wave took him away."

They both cried.

"She gave me the power to find you. I have your jade heart."

"You keep the heart...it brought you to me. Your father bought it for you when you were born. I was only meant to keep the heart only until you were older."

Amy touched the heart. It meant so much more to her now knowing that her father had picked it out himself.

"Grandmother is very powerful. Why didn't you turn to her for help?"

"When I left home I thought by taking your Papa away from New Orleans I was saving him. I didn't know Serena was his mother or I would have gone to her. She had the power to stop them. If I had only known...your Papa would be alive today. Your Papa loved you. He said he had known true happiness the day you were born."

"All these years I felt you close by, but not Papa. I prayed for you and Papa every night."

"Serena will watch out for you. Trust her."

"She turned all the ones that hurt Papa into rat people. They are frightfully ugly. They have a man's head, a rat's body and Jimmy told me they speak with this funny accent called Cajun."

Celeste smiled but, with sadness. "I have missed you every day but I thought you were gone. I'm coming home...I can't wait...soon."

Then the vision of Amy disappeared into the night. Celeste cried in joy for her daughter found but sadness for her husband lost forever. In her heart she had always known Philippe would have done everything in his power to find her if he was still alive. Now that her memory was restored she remembered the night the ship sank and Philippe giving up his seat next to her and then a wave took him away from her...forever.

Amy woke up but she knew it was not just a dream. Her Mother was coming home to her. Tears fell from her eyes when she thought about her Papa. Since that night on the sinking ship she hadn't felt his presence but to know that he had died that night in the Irish Sea was very sad and tore at her heart and soul. If she could just see him again.

Serena heard her plea.

The carriage settled under the porte-cochere.

Perkins helped Serena and then Amy exit into the courtyard.

Annie was just waking up.

"Annie, bring Jimmy inside when he wakes up."

"Awww."

"Don't pout. Miss Amy will be my guest for a while so you'll have plenty of time to show off your monkey tail."

"Okay."

Annie watched them leave and wondered how long Jimmy was going to nap.

She followed Serena into a small, cozy room. All dark wood bookcases with overstuffed chairs and ottomans. A wood fire burned in a stone fireplace flanked by wing chairs. One wall was glass and looked out to a courtyard lit with tiny lanterns.

"Not what you expected, is it?"

Amy smiled. "I imagined a huge mansion with tons of magical things inside and out."

The door opened and a very old woman entered the room pushing a heavy tea cart in front of her.

"Amy, this is Frieda, Perkins wife. Frieda is the world's best cook and a fantastic baker."

Frieda started to pour the tea.

"Thank you, Frieda. Please take care of Amy for a moment. I have something I have to do."

Amy had never seen so many wonderful sweets to eat as the ones that filled the two lower shelves of the tea cart. The top shelf held a silver tea service atop an ornately carved silver tray and a delicate porcelain tier of plates filled with little sandwiches.

Frieda poured a cup of tea and handed Amy a delicately flowered china plate indicating she could help herself.

Serena went into the courtyard to seek out her crystal ball, ignoring the storm around her. "My Darling,

Only this very day I received your note.
There has never been anyone but you, don't you see.

Hear my plea and come to me.
We have a son I know not where
Please find him and bring him home.

It was now in fate's hands, Serena thought as she hurried back inside.

Watching Amy enjoy the treats Frieda had made she wondered how the young girl stayed so slim. She remembered many years ago when she could eat anything, too.

Annie could smell Frieda's fabulous fruit pies and cakes in the air.

She looped her tail over the chandelier in the ceiling of the carriage and started swinging back and forth and upside down, but Jimmy just snored louder.

Annie started swinging harder making a loud creaking sound.

What is that awful noise, Jimmy thought. He sat up and was surprised to see a dog hanging by a monkey tail. Could things get any worse? They could. Amy was nowhere around.

"Hello there." He felt ridiculous bending over to talk to the dog.

"Oh, good. You're awake. The Mistress said I had to watch over you until you woke up and then bring you inside. That's where Miss Amy is, in case you are wondering."

Jimmy sat up straight.

"By the way, did you see any ghosts at that plantation?" Annie swung by her tail giving him a silly smile. "You haven't met Polly by any chance, have you?"

"No, I didn't see any ghosts, and who is Polly? Is that a ghost, too?"

"No, silly boy. For your information Polly is a large, very colorful Mexican parrot. Shame about the ghosts. I've always wanted to see one."

"Would this Polly have a broomstick, too?"

"I guess you didn't see her because if you had you would know she doesn't need a broomstick because she has very big wings. She's the kind that makes an impression, know what I mean? Anyway she'd be perched right here on the seat chattering about what a big storm there was earlier."

Jimmy really didn't know what to say. A talking parrot! He struggled to find common ground with Annie. "Is that a monkey's tail?"

Annie loved to show off. "It is. Grand, isn't it? Great for hanging around. You can have one, too, if you like. Just ask the Mistress."

"Thanks but I think I'll pass on that fashion accessory. I'm ready to go, if you are."

"By the way, I'm Annie." Annie uncurled her tail and dropped down with a bit of a thud. "Hard getting used to that but I'm working on it."

"I should think so." He didn't want to mention the strangeness of a dog having a monkey tail since she was, after all, a talking dog.

"Follow me." Annie led the way from the porte cochere into the house.

Amy hearing Jimmy in the hall called to him. "Come join us."

Jimmy welcomed the warmth of the fire while Annie curled up at Serena's feet.

"Jimmy, this is my Grandmother."

"Miss Serena, a lovely evening to you. I'd love to stay and chat but I better get home." What do they say, he thought, about the shorter the visitors stay the more they're welcomed back. But he couldn't help giving the tiers of sandwiches a very hungry look.

"Jimmy, you are incorrigible." Amy laughed.

He bowed to Serena. "Thank you for the rescue."

"Jimmy, don't be silly, sit down and have some tea with us." Serena glared at him wondering who would turn down Frieda's cakes and little sandwiches?

"I would love to but I have to go make things right with Marie. She's planning on picking us up in the morning from Devereux."

"We're going to Parkway at Hagan for hot roast beef po'boys. If you want to join us be here tomorrow at eleven."

"Wow! Thank you!"

"And tell Marie that Amy is with me and she'll be back when she gets there." Serena smiled.

"I will." With that Jimmy left thinking about the story he would tell his brothers about tonight.

"Thank you for your kindness to Jimmy."

Serena smiled at Amy. "My son loves going to Parkway on Hagan."

Annie had to get her bit in. "When Master Philippe was here we used to go all the time. The owner, Miss Eileen and the Mistress are friends. When they had a big hurricane a few years ago the Mistress waterproofed all their ovens and lifted them thirty feet into the air until the water went away."

"That was really a kind thing to do."

"My son would never have forgiven me if I hadn't saved his favorite restaurant." Serena smiled.

"Then it will be mine, too."

The soft rain outside became a downpour. When Amy lived at the Orphanage the air had a salty smell with an faint scent of rotting leaves in the fall but here the air was sweet and clean and smelled of night blooming Jasmine and Gardenias.

"I returned to New Orleans with Philippe. I built a hunting lodge, the big house, on Esplanade in the hopes that Philippe's father would return to us. It was a house fit for a man. Dark wood, large rooms each with a fireplace. A wide staircase leading to the second floor. I had a staff of ten who occupied rooms on the upper floors. The gardens were extensive and led right down to the water."

Amy started to ask when her father was born but she wasn't sure if she wanted to find out that it might be hundreds of years ago.

Serena continued. "I was very much in love with Philippe's father. He was Jean Lafitte, you know. I heard that Lafitte's ship was sunk off the Florida Keys. I always held out hope that just once he would see his son. The years passed and never a word. Philippe grew tall and strong like his father. When Philippe left with your mother I was very lonely."

"But you could have found him and brought him

back." "He told me he would return one day."

"I loved my papa very much." Amy whispered.

"I cursed the Claiborne family and I turned the Boudreaux boys, who had hurt my son, into rat people. The lodge was much too big for me after Philippe left so I built this house and moved here."

"What about the curse?"

Serena smiled gently at Amy. "I took away the curse many years ago. It was done in a fit of anger and I'm sorry I did it."

"What a relief! But I'm glad my Aunt Lily didn't know that because I'm pretty sure she would never have brought me back here."

Lily Claiborne rang a bell summoning Glory into her room. Glory was anxious since the old woman had rarely spoken to her in the many years she had worked in the house.

She knocked gently on Lily's bedroom door.

"Come in." Lily's big booming voice terrified Glory even more.

"Mistress. Is there anything I can do?"

"Stupid girl. I wouldn't have called you here if there wasn't."

"Thank you, Mistress." Glory curtsied and felt foolish doing so but it seemed to appease the Mistress for the time being.

"I can't find Marie. Where is she?" Lily demanded in a stern voice that made Glory shake with fear.

"I don't know, Mistress but I will find her for you."

"Do that and have her come to my room at once. And don't take all day about it."

Glory didn't want to point out that it was eleven o'clock at night but how could she point out the time of day to someone who never opened the heavy drapes in her room.

Relieved, she quickly left the room. When she got back to the kitchen she called Marie on her private number that only she and Melita had. "Oh, thank goodness I found you. Miss Lily wants to see you right away."

"Thank you, Glory. Did she say what she wanted?"

"No, she just said she couldn't find you and I was to do that and tell you to come to her room right away."

Marie hung up the phone and hurried down the stairs from the small apartment above the Carriage House to Lily's chambers.

Marie knocked lightly on Lily's door. She wished she was anywhere but here right now.

"Marie, don't just stand out there, come on in!"

Marie walked in and quietly shut the door behind her. "Where is that bratty child?" "Sleeping."

Marie had just talked to Jimmy on the phone and she knew that Amy was with Serena but she was definitely not going to tell Lily where she was. And Amy was not a bratty child. It was getting harder and harder to hold her tongue around this disagreeable woman.

"The minute the Pirates Ball is over I want her out of this house. She will have served her purpose."

"Where will she go?" Marie was horrified.

"Not my problem. Put her on a cargo boat and ship her back to Scotland. Those cargo boats take cheap fare passengers, so I've heard."

"Yes, Madame."

Marie turned and left the room before she started crying.

"More tea?"

Amy yawned. "Yes. Thank you."

Serena poured a cup and turned to hand it to Amy. Not to her surprise Amy was fast asleep. She pulled a sash that rang a bell in the kitchen.

"It has been a long day, Ma Petite."

Amy reluctantly opened one eye. "Oh, I'm fine. Where were we?"

"You were on your way to bed."

Frieda appeared in the doorway.

"Is the room ready for my granddaughter?"

"It is."

"Do not worry about Marie." "I
was just thinking about her."

Serena smiled. "She has been told. We have a big day ahead of us tomorrow."

The next day Jimmy woke up at five o'clock. He started to go back to sleep but then he remembered that this was a special day. In just a few hours he'd be hanging out with the Black Witch! The thought certainly got him going.

He became a whirlwind of activity. He straightened his room first then moved into the living room, the kitchen and the game room with The Pirate Treasure Game waiting for them to resume playing. Wouldn't it be fantastic, he thought, if she came back here and honored them a quick game? Well...he could ask, couldn't he?

Just as he dusted the game board, which he had never done before, the treasure chest flew open and gave him a good what for!

"Hey, get a life. When was the last time you cleaned this board? Wait....let me answer that.....NEVER!!!!" The chest screamed and with the screeching laugh of a maniac the lid slammed shut and sea water started sloshing off the table and on the floor in a frightening manner.

"Sorry! Sorry! I won't do it again!"

Jimmy ran out of the room before the place was flooded.

He raced through the tunnel, slowing only to give a quick look at the secret door leading to Amy's room, but he knew she was at Serena's so he kept going.

Exiting in the hotel's garden, he was surprised to find the staff setting up for a costume contest which would start that afternoon and last until the judging on Mardi Gras Day.

The hotel staff wouldn't let him leave until he promised he would bring Amy back for the party.

"I can't promise anything but I might bring her grandmother, too, if that's okay."

"Sure, the more the merrier."

Wait until they meet Amy's grandmother, Jimmy thought with a smile. It was almost eleven o'clock and he had a feeling Serena was a stickler for promptness.

CHAPTER TEN

Amy's Reunited With Her Mom

"The front door! Someone get the front door, please!" Lily screamed from her bedroom right off the entry.

Marie hurried to the door, wiping her hands on a dust cloth. It couldn't be Amy since she was safe with Serena.

She immediately recognized the lovely woman standing there. Marie would have known her anywhere. She dropped her dust cloth and rushed to give her a big hug. "Oh, Celeste, I am so happy to see you! I knew you were still alive somewhere! Amy did, too. She's a wonderful young girl."

"Marie, I am so glad to see you. Thank you for finding her. I have a million things to tell you but right now I want to see Amy."

"Yes. Yes." Marie rushed her inside out of the cold. Forgetting to speak in a whisper she blurted out loud, "I have so much to tell you."

Lily, who couldn't bear to miss out on anything, yelled, "Marie, who is it?"

"I want to see Amy. Is she here?" Celeste spoke in a low voice to Marie, not sure how Lily would greet her.

Before Marie could answer Lily threw open her bedroom door.

"Well, well, it's Celeste. I'm not surprised. Just in time for the Pirate's Ball, are we?"

"Lily!" Celeste wanted to rush to Lily but was stopped by the look of hatred on her sister's face. Lily had never been friendly towards her when they were growing up but she didn't remember her as being this cruel. "I have so much to tell you but first I want to see my daughter. Amy and I have been separated for many years."

"She's probably still asleep. And I really don't care what you have to tell me."

Marie spoke up. "She's not here. She's with her grandmother."

"Her grandmother! What grandmother?" Lily was shocked at this news. "You lied to me! You said she was in her bedroom, sleeping." Lily gave Marie such a horrible look Marie would have withered if Celeste hadn't been there. Lily snarled, "I will deal with you later." If Lily decided to be accommodating until after the Ball she wasn't any longer.

"Get out, Celeste! You are not welcome in my house."

"But it's my home." Celeste felt the waves of hatred coming from her sister.

"Not any more. After seven years I had you legally declared dead. Everything is now mine and I repeat you are not welcome here."

Melita and Glory, hearing the horrible shouting, stood quietly in the shadows at the end of the hall.

Marie took Celeste's arm. "Lily, repeating what you told me last night that Amy is to be put out in the street after she reigns as Pirate Queen, then I'm leaving with Celeste."

Melita and Glory took their chance to get out of this terrible house.

"We're going, too." They chimed in together.

"All of you get out! I don't need any of you. It will be easy enough to find help."

"Not likely." Glory whispered loud enough for everyone to hear.

"Melita, Glory, get your things and meet me in front. Quickly now." Marie said to the two women who looked panic stricken when the reality of their circumstances came through.

Marie took Celeste's arm and led her up the stairs.

"Where are you going?" Lily was furious.

"We're getting Amy's things. We'll be gone shortly."

Melita and Glory, right behind them, continued on to the attic to pack.

While Celeste gathered Amy's few clothes into the bag she had brought from the orphanage Marie phoned Marcel. "Pack all our things. Don't forget the envelope taped behind the chest of drawers. And get our car ready. Melita and Glory are coming with us, too.

"Lily fired you?" Marcel asked in amazement.

"No, I quit. We all quit. I'll tell you all about it. Just be ready for us when we come out."

Amy had only a few things so it was easy to pack her things. Marie added the photograph album that had pictures of Celeste when she was young.

They all left the house under a hateful glare from Lily.

Marcel was waiting in front. He loaded their luggage into the trunk of a very old Ford.

Everyone piled into the car, Marie and Celeste in the front, Melita and Glory in the back.

"Serena has a house on Esplanade, right? Philippe once told me he lived there with his Mother." Celeste was trying to remember her late night talks with Philippe.

"That house still stands but Serena left when...anyway she has another place on Toulouse. That's where we're going."

While Marie gave directions to the house on Toulouse, Celeste looked out the window at the French Quarter, a place she thought she'd never return to.

They drove into a two story garage marked *Private Club Parking Only.*

Celeste didn't remember this garage being here.

They approached an opening in a stucco wall just large enough for any size vehicle to pass through and paused in the middle for five seconds before driving on.

They emerged into Pirate Village.

"Where are we?" Celeste was amazed.

Seamus had just come out of the shower when his cell phone rang. He checked the time on his phone. It was close to Noon.

"Angus here. I'm at the Devereux dock on the Mississippi. How soon can ye get to the dock?"

"Ye're on a boat?"

"Kind of."

"I'll be right there."

Seamus disconnected and remembered that the ugly Cajun rat left from the dock last night. He wondered what Angus had done with his car.

He quickly dressed in his now cleaned and dried clothes and made sure he pocketed the few things he came with. He found Miss Devereux having brunch and heartily thanked her for her kind hospitality. Passing on the offer of anything to eat, he asked directions before he hurried down the path towards the River.

He could see Angus' old car strapped down on the top of a barge. A towboat was discharging large amounts of smoke while trying to keep the barge near the dock without knocking it down.

Seamus leaped onto the deck of the barge and Angus shouted out, "Take off, Cap!"

The towboat pulled the barge into the Mississippi current headed for New Orleans.

"Angus, ye are a man with an imagination."

Angus laughed. "Aye, comes in handy if ye live around here."

Marie smiled. "I see the Claiborne's never told you about Pirate Village."

"Where's the private club? We went through an arch in the parking lot that said something about a private club and what is Pirate Village? Is that in the French Quarter?" Had the French Quarter changed so much since she'd been gone?

"Well to begin with, just to get here you have to have pirate blood running through your veins. You have Blackbeard in your family history. Melita and Glory are descendants of Black Bart. In the 1800s a female pirate by the name of Anne was captain of her own ship. Marcel came from her family tree. And I have the blood line of the only Irish Leprechaun who swabbed the deck on one of Lafitte's galleons." Marie smiled. This was a lot for Celeste to take in all at once.

"You're a Leprechaun?"

Marcel smiled at Marie and just kept driving.

"Let's say I come from a branch of the family. Now as to Pirate Village...there are tons of real pirates all over the place. Over there is the Pirate Savings and Loan, the Pirate Café, Pirate Gifts and Things. Pirate Park has a huge area with rides on pirate ships, treasure hunts on Treasure Island, and summer camp for wannabe young pirates, which is great fun. There is an extraordinary ride on a glass enclosed pirate ship that goes over sand dunes, through caves and underwater exploring sunken pirate ships with treasure chests that have spilled their loot of emeralds, rubies, diamonds, gold and pieces of eight. Just tons of fun things to do."

Celeste just sat there looking amazed.

"I can see all this will take a long time to explain but we're at Serena's house. You are going to finally meet your daughter, who will reign as Queen of the Pirates Ball."

Celeste was out of the car first, followed by Marie.

As they walked to the front door Celeste looked worried. "Do you think she will remember me, Marie?"

"Of course, a child never forgets her Mother."

Since Jimmy had just arrived, and was still in the entry when Marie pulled up in front, he opened the door when Serena called out "Will somebody get the door. It's busier this morning than it's been the past one hundred and fifty years!"

One hundred and fifty years, Amy thought. She wanted to ask her grandmother to explain that but it's impolite to ask a lady her age.

When she heard Marie say "Jimmy, this is Celeste" Amy forgot all the questions she wanted to ask her Grandmother. Her mother was here! She had been hoping for this moment for thirteen long years. "Mama," she cried when they were still feet apart. Closing the distance Amy ran into Celeste's open arms.

Like Marie said...a child never forgets her own Mother.

Jimmy stood there wondering if he was ever going to get his roast beef po'boy and then felt incredibly guilty for thinking of food at a time like this. He turned to Marie. "This is turning out to be one incredible day."

"You have no idea." Marie rolled her eyes.

"Mama, are you cold, there's a fire in the great room. Are you hungry? I have prayed for this moment for so long! Please tell me where you have been. What happened to you? I have so much to tell you."

"I was told everyone from the ship had drowned. I thought it was true. How could any child survive in the rough sea that night? As the high waves took you away I could see someone bailing water out of the lifeboat you were in. I believed them when they said you were gone. But every night, in the dark when I closed my eyes, I could sense you were nearby. I prayed this day would come."

"Mama, I have so much to tell you but first come meet Grandmother. She is wonderful."

Amy took her mother's hand like she never wanted to let it go.

Jimmy and Marie followed behind them.

"How did Lily take all this?" Jimmy whispered.

The look Marie gave him said everything.

"That bad, huh?"

"Worse." Marie looked grim.

"Grandmother, this is my Mom."

Serena held out her hand. Her smile was warm and welcoming as the huge wood fire blazing in the room.

"My dear, we meet. Please call me Serena."

"Thank you. Philippe told me so much about you that I feel I know you."

"And Grandmother, this is Marie. I told you about her. She brought me back from the Orphanage and watched over me."

"Please, everyone, sit. Amy is very dear to me so anyone she calls a friend is one to me."

Celeste sat on a small sofa next to Amy. Perkins brought extra chairs into the room.

"Marie, please sit. I heard this morning was very difficult for all of you."

Marie spoke quickly. "Celeste came to the house. Lily was terribly mean. She said she was the owner of the house now and told Celeste to leave and never come back. I said if Celeste wasn't welcome then I was leaving. I was distraught the night before when Lily told me that after the ball she was throwing Amy out. Melita and Glory, the cook and the housekeeper said they were leaving, too. They are waiting in the car outside with my husband. I want to stay but right now I have to go. We need to find a place to live."

"So the Claiborne's are still throwing people, and now family, out in the street?"

"I think that's a good description."

"That is wonderful news. I have a perfect home for everyone. My dear Amy, you and your Mother will have a huge house that requires staff so Marie, your husband, Melita and Glory will have much better jobs there and wonderful accommodations, too."

"Oh, Grandmother, I'd never be any trouble to you."

"How would you be any trouble to me? You and your mother are my family now. We'll go at once to the house on Esplanade. It's been closed up for too long. Your father loved it there. He called it The Lodge." Serena smiled, gently remembering.

Celeste touched Serena's arm. "Thank you. Philippe loved you dearly. I now know why. If he could just see how you have welcomed us...."

Serena patted the soft hand touching her arm. "He knows."

Rising, she called out. "Perkins, get the car ready. Bring Frieda. We are going to The Lodge."

Marie, Melita and Glory climbed into the car with Marcel and Frieda.

"We'll follow you." Marie called out. As soon as she got in the car she quickly brought her husband up to date on what was going on.

Amy, Celeste and Jimmy went with Serena. Perkins, as always, drove.

It was a short drive to Esplanade which was a grand Avenue with the oldest of houses and the tallest of oak trees in the French Quarter. The mansions along the wide Avenue had servant's quarters on the third and fourth floors. Many were made of St. Louis brick with heart of pine floors, large fireplaces and twelve foot ceilings. Many had summer kitchens in the backyard which kept the cooking heat outside the houses making the inside only a bit cooler from June to December.

Number 12 Esplanade was one such large mansion. The cedar shingles had weathered silver grey over centuries past.

Everyone piled into the coolness of the entryway.

Amy and her Mom stayed close to Serena while they walked from room to room. Marie and Jimmy were thrilled testing the antique furniture for comfort.

Melita and Glory went back and forth helping Marcel and Perkins carry in all the luggage.

Frieda went to check out the kitchen and make a grocery list of things they would need.

Serena hadn't been here in years yet the place looked lived in and comfortable. The rooms seemed to be holding their collective breath hoping for a kind word and that was just what they got.

"I had forgotten how wonderfully large, yet intimate, the house is." Serena looked around. She could almost hear the house sigh in contentment. "There are two en suite bedrooms on the first floor one at each end of the house, four bedrooms on the second floor and six bedrooms on the third floor. I used to have a large staff that occupied the top floors, which has its own separate staircase to the kitchen."

"This is a really beautiful house. Thank you. I know I speak for all of us." Marie felt right at home.

Serena smiled. "Frieda will show you everything and answer all your questions."

"We will start in the kitchen." Frieda led Melita and Glory out of the room. Marie followed.

Marcel, having found the staircase to the third floor, was quite busy hauling all the luggage upstairs.

"Grandmother, I forgot to thank you so very much for everything."

"My darling, Amy, I meant what I said about family. There is nothing to thank me for. Now...I think I've had you to myself long enough. You and your Mother have much to talk about."

"We do! A lifetime."

"Jimmy, let's go." Serena started walking towards the front door.

"Oh yes indeed!" Jimmy hurried along behind her. "Uh, go? Go where?"

"To get that po'boy you've been drooling about."

Perkins was already out the door waiting for his Mistress to turn the car into a carriage. With the heavy Mardi Gras traffic it was the only way to go.

Jimmy hurried as fast as he could, grumbling all the way. He was still complaining, very quietly, when he got to the car and opened the door. "I do not drool."

"I don't drool, either." Annie added from her seat by the window.

"Oh, good grief! How did this get started?"

Jimmy was so fascinated with the flying carriage that he forgot to complain all the way to the landing in City Park, a private location close to the most famous po'boy restaurant in New Orleans, Fairway at Hagen.

"Gerald, did you see that?" Mildred was looking up just as the black carriage flew by and hovered in a clearing beyond the trees. She had a good view from the path where they walked their little dog.

"Hurry up, Bruno!" Gerald jerked on his leash.

Bruno, a little English Bulldog, was going to take his good time and nobody was going to rush him. Gerald was mean to him but he put up it because he loved his daily walk through the park. And he always stopped at the concrete bench on the path they took every day. Bruno checked out the different smells. All his friends stopped here, too.

"Gerald?"

"See what, Mildred?" He said in a voice that showed just how bored he was with everything and especially with her.

Mildred watched as a large black car emerged from the meadow ringed by a dense forest of trees. She could swear the opening in the trees closed behind the car as it passed.

"A flying carriage! It landed somewhere in the forest and..." For one second her boring life came alive with an expectation of adventure.

"Mildred, there is definitely something wrong with you." Gerald laughed in a very cruel manner.

"But you were looking right at it!"

"All I saw was a whole bunch of scraggly looking trees."

"But—"

"Let's go. I don't have all day to spend walking Bruno. I have important things to do."

"Yes, Gerald." She wondered what was important. He was an Engineer who often took jobs out of the country, leaving her behind. But when he wasn't working he sat in his recliner all day watching television and yelling for her to bring him beer and snacks.

Mildred, as usual, said nothing and walked meekly behind him.

On their return Gerald was pulled off the path by Bruno, who wanted to stop by his favorite concrete bench again just to check out any new smells...it was a social thing. Gerald let him since he wanted to sit down. He pulled out a newspaper he had folded in a side pocket of his jacket and started to read.

Mildred, ignored as usual, wandered towards the place where earlier she had seen the large black car. She could hear the crinkle of paper, the kind you wrap food in, before she reached the clearing. The black car she had seen earlier was there. The windows were down and she could hear music and laughter coming from inside.

Suddenly the air around the meadow shimmered. Time stopped.

The black car turned into a black carriage pulled by four black horses with black ostrich plumes on their heads. The horses reared up and the carriage lifted high into the air, disappearing into a mist that seemed to surround it.

Mildred felt lost, like she had just missed out on something very exciting.

Walking back to the concrete bench she found Gerald looking, as usual, very irritated with everything she did.

"Well, did you find your flying carriage?" He mocked her.

"I did! That large black car turned into a beautiful carriage and it flew off."

"Right. I suggest next time we go to Preservation Hall you refrain from having a Hurricane because they're starting to make you go daft."

"Let's go, Bruno." Gerald pulled Bruno along.

It hurt her soul to see Gerald mistreat Bruno. She loved the little dog. She followed behind them towards their modest little house and their boring little life. She wished her life was different.

Mildred was lonely.

Serena heard her plea. With a twist of her wrist and a snap of her fingers she gave Mildred a very amazing gift...imagination.

Mildred would never be lonely again.

While Bubba was waiting for everyone to show up he started imagining just how his plan would play out. Perfectly, that's how!

"Bubba, yoo-hoo! We're all here."

"Excellent. Okay, here is the game plan. Beau, listen up, while everyone is outside in the reviewing stands you will give Mickey a note from Amy asking him to meet her on the third floor by the bathrooms. The note will say she needs help carrying something to the car."

A little rat paw shot up.

"Yes, Tommy."

"What's she got that she wants carried?"

Bubba put a paw up to his forehead. He was in the midst of a bunch of morons. All he could do was just hope this went off successfully.

"She doesn't have anything to carry. She'll be in the stands toasting her King. The idea is to get Mickey upstairs into the third floor hallway where Beau will knock him out. Got it?"

"Yes, thank you."

"Okay. Now Beau, as I said, while Queen Amy is toasting her King from the stands you hand Mickey the note then race up to the third floor and hide in the dark hallway. When Mickey gets there knock him out, drag him into the bathroom, tie him up and tape his mouth. Oh, and don't forget to hang a sign on the outside of the bathroom door saying *Out of Order Until after Mardi Gras.* And very important...don't forget to pick up Mickey's chauffeur's cap. You now will look like him. Return to the limo and get in. You have to appear ready to take Queen Amy to the auditorium. Traditionally she will be alone."

Another little rat paw shot up in the air.

Bubba wanted to scream but a little rat scream is stupid and wouldn't accomplish anything right now.

"Yes, Jacques!"

"What if someone is with her?"

"If there's a court lady or two with her we'll just improvise. Okay?"

"Qui."

Bubba thought Jacques took the Cajun French thing a little too far but now was not the time to go into that. Once he was back looking like a man again he planned on hiding in the Bayou. He had a thousand hiding places where no one would find him, especially his imbecile brothers.

"Cousin Buck will fix the door locks on the car while Beau is taking care of Mickey. Right Cousin Buck?"

"Tommy's tiny rat paw shot up again."

Bubba bit his lip to keep from screaming. "Yes, Tommy, what is it?"

"What is Bucky doing to the door locks?"

"I know I explained this to you before but here it is. He's going to fix the locks so when Queen Amy gets in the back seat the doors lock and she can't get them open."

Tommy's paw once again started to go up in the air but Bubba had enough. "SHUT UP! "SHUT UP!" He turned back to Buck trying to regain his composure. "Buck are we on the same page?"

Buck nodded vigorously. He was just glad he and Beau were normal size men because they were running out of family volunteers who wanted to help the brothers.

Bubba went over it one more time for the idiots in the room. "When Beau gets back to the limo he'll get in and make sure the doors lock after Amy gets into the back seat. The car doors won't be able to open. Then Beau will let the rest of us into the front seat and he'll drive off, headed for a secret place in the bayou, where we will keep her until Serena changes us all back to our human bodies. If Serena doesn't change us back we'll threaten to kill her precious Amy. She will do anything we say."

Bubba rushed to add when he saw the look on his brother's faces. "Of course we're not going to kill anybody. We just want to threaten that we will."

"Good plan!"

A chorus of yahoo and hand clapping by Beau followed.

Donny raised his weak little rat paw.

"Yes, Donny?"

"Where will we be during all this?"

"We'll be watching from a city trash can close by in case something goes wrong, which I do not expect to happen if we all do what we're supposed to do. Got it?"

An excited chorus of YES went up from the Cajun rats.

The Boudreaux brothers, along with cousin Beau and cousin Buck, all went home after the meeting feeling like they had an excellent plan in place, nothing would go wrong and the brothers would be turned back into real men in a few days. They were going to sleep well tonight.

Just as the French Quarter came into view a large, colorful parrot flew through the open window of the carriage smacking Jimmy in the face with one large wing and settled on the seat next to him.

Jimmy screamed while spitting bird feathers out of his mouth.

"Oh for Heaven's sakes, Jimmy, it's only Polly." Serena smiled.

"Hello." Jimmy wrinkled his nose at the parrot wondering if the articles he'd read online about parrot fever were true. God only knows where this bird had been anyway.

"No! Parrots don't have any kind of fever! At least I don't!" Polly glared back at him.

Jimmy was upset that she could read his mind. "What kind of silly name is Polly anyway? What a cliché like *Polly, wanna a cracker?*"

"Yeah...well...well...look at those ridiculous shoes you're wearing and that silly hat. You're a walking cliché for an Irish Leprechaun!"

"You're just a bunch of feathers flying in formation." He stuck his tongue out at her.

Serena had been talking on her cell phone and had missed the ridiculous exchange going on, until now.

"Stop it! Both of you! Polly, you are inches away from going back to being a raccoon about to drown in the pond in my courtyard. And Jimmy, you are two giant Simon says steps away from being a stucco yard gnome. Get along, you two!"

The minute Serena looked away Jimmy made big circles around his eyes with his thumb and forefingers reminding Polly of the raccoon comment Serena had made.

Polly started to wail. "He's making fun of me. He's making fun of me!"

Serena sat there wondering just when had she turned into the Headmistress of a Nursery School.

Polly and Jimmy bickered, discreetly, nonstop until the carriage, made invisible by its own cloud, landed on top of The Golden Palace."

"I have a dreadful headache." Serena held a hand to her forehead. "I'm going home to bed. See you later, Jimmy."

Remembering his manners Jimmy got out and gave Serena an elegant bow. "Thank you. That was a wonderful picnic. Maybe one day you might visit. I have three brothers who would love to play The Pirate Treasure Game with you."

"My favorite! We'll do that soon."

As the carriage started to lift off Jimmy saw Polly plastered to the window and he gave the same evil eye to her as she was giving him.

Frieda met the carriage at the Toulouse house.

"They are very busy over at the Lodge. Amy and her Mother are still talking, talking, talking. Can I get you anything?"

"Frieda, I need a good rest." Serena laughed. Even Immortals get tired."

Polly flew into the courtyard. She had a favorite perch in the top of the tree. She was really disappointed. She finally had a chance to talk to Jimmy, who she thought was someone from England, and he had turned out to be a total dud. London was a secret place she had always wanted to visit. And to see the Queen would be a dream come true! How in the world would a Mexican jungle parrot get to London?

In just a few days Polly would find out. In just a few days she'd be in this very carriage flying fast across the ocean to the city she had always wanted to visit.

Amy, Queen of the Pirates Ball

CHAPTER ELEVEN
Alligator- On- A- Stick Is On The Menu

"Get up, get up, you sleepyhead....it's a wonderful day in Leprechaun City!"

A little clock shouted out as it jiggled about on Jimmy's end table. It rang bells and three tiny Leprechauns leaped out of the clock and danced an Irish Jig while singing "Oh, Jimmy Boy." They changed the Danny to Jimmy.

Jimmy pulled a pillow over his head which irritated the little Irish dancers. Thinking with one mind they leaped off the table and landed on the top of Jimmy's chest where they started poking him with their Walking Sticks.

Jimmy roared and the little dancers leaped off his chest and scattered around the room shouting "Ha, ha, ha, you can't catch us....you can't catch us!"

The clock jiggled with laughter and leaped off the end table with a blaring alarm. Jimmy finally tackled the fast moving clock and turned off the alarm. It was nine o'clock.

He groaned. They were overdue at LouLou's for Amy's final gown fitting.

He dressed in record time, grabbed a piece of cold toast in the kitchen and stuffed it into his pocket.

Now he had a major problem. He'd never make it to the Lodge on foot. This was the day before Mardi Gras! Throngs of people would be in the streets.

Jimmy had an idea. He grabbed a rocket pack and protective eye goggles from the hall closet and a banner that attached to his shoulders like a cape that trailed out behind him. It said **Welcome to Mardi Gras.** He had to use the banner or tourists would be panicked at the sight of a flying Leprechaun. With the banner everyone would think he was a remote controlled flying object. He put on a jacket that held the rocket controls.

On numerous occasions the Mayor of New Orleans had hired him to strap on his double rocket pack and fly around trailing a banner advertising some convention group or a new restaurant.

He raced down the tunnel, through the garden of The Golden Palace and took an elevator to the rooftop. On the way to the roof he zipped up his jacket and strapped on his rocket pack.

The rooftop was empty, which was great since he wasn't sure how he would explain flying off into the sky with rockets on his back. He turned the power knob on the front of his windbreaker to the right. The rockets ignited with a blast of fire, lifting him straight up in the bright blue sky and away he flew trailing his advertising banner.

Looking down, he was glad he did not have to make his way through the crowds in the street below.

One very astounded tourist nudged his wife and shouted, "Look! Up in the sky! It's one of those advertising remote things and it's using a Leprechaun!"

"Ralph, I told you once if I told you a million times...you need glasses. Where? I don't see anything. Anyway they have a lot of Irish here. They named a part of the city The Irish Channel...it says so right here in the guide book!"

By the time Ralph's wife was finished reading him the riot act Jimmy had arrived at the Lodge.

Landing was tricky. He had to turn the power knob to the left and slowly lose power so he could land softly, feet first.

Once he wasn't paying attention and turned the power knob the wrong way upon landing. He caught the mistake before he ended up spinning into the ground so hard he would end up in China.

Jimmy landed gently on the front lawn and rushed to knock on the door. He was late. It was the fault of that stupid alarm clock.

He didn't have time to unstrap the rocket pack before Amy threw the door open with a bright smile and a laugh as she looked him up and down. "Love the costume! She looked at the banner lying in a crumpled heap on the pathway behind him. "Dropped your flag!" She called over her shoulder, "Mom, ready to go?" And then stepped aside for Jimmy to enter.

Grumbling, he snatched the *"Welcome to Mardi Gras"* banner off the ground. It was starting to look a bit frayed. "It's not a flag, it's a banner! And this is not a costume it's my rocket pack."

The last caught Amy's attention. She was fascinated as she watched him stash his jacket with the controls, the rock pack and goggles in the hall closet. He stuffed the banner on top of everything.

"Those really are rockets. Did you fly here?"

"I did."

"How exciting! Would you show me how to fly around one day?"

"Oh, sure!" Jimmy dramatically flung his hands into the air. "You could take it for a spin and soar up in the air dashing here and there, up and down....NO!"

"Jimmy, sometimes you are no fun!"

"We're late. Let's go."

Celeste joined them and they set out on foot.

Due to the huge crowds they got to LouLou's one hour later.

LouLou, wearing a very colorful dress was sitting on the stoop in front of her shotgun double watching the tourists go by.

"Figured with the crowds it would take ya'll longer. Ya'll made it okay, I see."

"LouLou, this is my mom." Amy proudly pointed this out but LouLou had immediately recognized Amy's mom, they looked like sisters.

LouLou laughed. "How's it goin' Celeste. Last time I saw you I was taking your measurements for a ball gown and then you up and disappeared on me."

"I'm sorry, LouLou."

"No mind about that. I've been saving that dress hoping you would come back one day. Figure you could use it tomorrow night, if you have a mind to."

"Oh, LouLou. I do indeed. I wouldn't miss it."

"Let's go on in and while Miss Amy is checking out her Queen's gown I'll go find yours."

They followed LouLou inside except for Jimmy who insisted on waiting outside. "Girl stuff." He grumbled.

"Amy, try on your gown. I'm gonna go look for your Mom's gown."

Carefully taking her gown off the padded hanger she dropped her jeans and sweatshirt in a corner and slipped the dress over her head.

It was made of soft gold silk and billowed all the way down to the floor. It had a waist cinching bodice made of gold silk with gold ribbon cords. It was a perfect fit. The second hanger held a long train made of gold silk brocade edged with ermine that attached at her shoulders. She felt like a Queen.

Amy released her black hair from the usual braid she wore and let it flow freely over her shoulders and down her back.

"Jimmy, come see."

Jimmy grumbled as he hopped off the stoop in front and climbed the stairs. He opened the door and stood there speechless. He wanted to tell her she looked like a pirate queen on a romance book cover but he didn't know what to say without babbling and looking ridiculous.

"You look nice." He turned and went back outside to continue his tourist watching from the front stoop.

Celeste and LouLou came back into the room. Celeste was wearing a beautiful gown of ivory lace over satin. The gown was floor length and had a high collar and long sleeves.

Celeste smiled. "Oh, Amy, you are beautiful." She stood beside her daughter who was looking into a three way mirror.

Amy didn't know what to say. She was definitely not used to having anyone tell her she was beautiful. Things like appearances were never talked about at the orphanage. She'd have to get used to this new world she was in.

"Mom, thank you." Amy was uncharacteristically shy. "Your gown is perfect."

"They were so conservative thirteen years ago." Celeste laughed. "Look at the long sleeves and high collar!"

"I bet LouLou could take off the sleeves and change the neckline." Amy was sure of that as she turned to the seamstress.

"No, no. I'm very happy with my gown. LouLou told me she will personally take the dresses to the Lodge this afternoon. Also your tiara and scepter."

"LouLou, thank you!" Amy was thrilled since that solved the problem of what to do with everything for the rest of the day.

Celeste left the room with LouLou trailing after her.

Once she undid the ribbons in the front that cinched in her waist to an amazingly small size her gown was much easier to get out of. She hung it back on the padded hanger, along with the train, and was sitting on the stoop outside with Jimmy when Celeste joined them.

"See ya'll later." LouLou waved from the front door.

Jimmy had been thinking about all the places to show Amy's mom. From her surprise about the changes in the Quarter he knew she didn't know about the other side of the brick wall. "How about a little tour of Pirate Village?"

"Where is that?"

Amy laughed. "Wait until you see the pirate ships and there's a gift shop that sells The Pirate Treasure Game.

Jimmy has one. We all played it at his house. Do you think we could stop and see it?"

"We'll take the grand tour. Let's start here." Jimmy opened the door to the Sweet Shop and Amy and Celeste went inside. He led them to the storeroom and showed Celeste how to place her hand on the brick wall and the door appeared. Jimmy opened the door and they walked through to the other side.

"Where are we?" Celeste remembered Pirates Alley but this place was totally different.

Jimmy explained. "This is Pirate Village and you can only get here if you have a pirate in your family tree."

Celeste looked around in wonder. She had no idea a Pirate Village existed inside the French Quarter.

"I guess your parents didn't introduce you to this pirate wonderland. I think they would rather forget that Blackbeard, or any pirate, was in your family tree. Do you hear the clink of coins in your pockets? The minute you passed through the wall, all your money was converted into pieces of eight, which you use for everything here. When we go back you will have your dollars, minus expenses taken out, returned to you."

"Oh, Mom, this is the most exciting place in the world. We went to Treasure Island on this big pirate ship and we stayed in a wonderful cave hotel, well wonderful...minus the smoke...and then we followed a map and found pirates treasure and we took a ride on a pirate ship that went over sand dunes, through caves, and under the ocean to see a sunken galleon with chests broken open spilling emeralds, rubies, diamonds and lots of gold." Amy was breathless with the excitement of reliving their adventures. "The only problem was that we sprung a leak but Jimmy rescued us with his magic gold dust!"

"Is that true" Celeste turned to Jimmy.

"Sort of. The true part was the leak and we were there. Unfortunately my magic gold dust doesn't work in or under water. I think your grandmother had a very big part in saving us, everyone else and the pirate ship."

"I had no idea." Amy smiled. "She really is my fairy godmother, too."

Celeste whispered, "I didn't know. She could have taken care of those horrible Cajun boys and we would never have left town."

"Mom, grandmother had her revenge on them. Jimmy told me she turned them into Cajun rats. They have the body of a large rat and the face of a Cajun man and they speak English with, what Jimmy tells me is, a Cajun accent. They must look really freaky."

Jimmy had been guiding them while they talked. "Ladies, we are at The Pirate Cafe where we can get alligator on a stick.

The streets in Pirate Village were nowhere as crowded as the other side of the wall.

"Oooh, I can't wait."

They left the café and tossed their now empty wood skewers in the trash.

"So what do you think?"

"Tastes just like chicken." Amy and her mom said at the same time and started laughing.

"I have an idea. Let's take mom to see The Pirate Treasure Game."

"Right this way." Jimmy led the way down the street.

He did not miss that someone was following them who looked exactly like Buck Boudreaux, or one of the lot with that characteristic pushed in piggy nose. Buck had been leaning against a doorway, a few doors down, when they excited the café and pushed off staying behind them as they walked towards The Gift Shop.

Jimmy purposefully stopped to look in the shop window so he could observe the stranger.

"Celeste, the game board can also be played outside."

Buck waited across the street, watching them with a very intent look on his face.

While Jimmy casually watched him, Amy was giving her mom a good description of how to play the game.

Jimmy waved as Aunt Maggie made her way through the crowd.

"Amy, look who's here!"

Amy's face lit up in a big smile. "Mom, this is Aunt Maggie. This is my Mom. Isn't it wonderful she's here!"

"It is truly a pleasure to see you again, Celeste. I had no idea."

Celeste took Maggie's hands in hers. "Maggie, I didn't think Amy made it. I couldn't be happier. They are giving me the grand tour. Please join us. Jimmy said something about the Boardwalk Over The Bayou Tour."

"I would love to, my dear." Maggie took Celeste's arm and the two ladies strolled ahead of Amy and Jimmy.

"Do we go on a boat in the bayou?"

"Yes, but first we take a boardwalk over the water. There are many exciting things to see in the bayou. It will lead us to the dock."

"Sounds like fun!" Amy was ready for anything.

They approached a ride that had a wooden path with railings on each side. Heavy fog kept them from seeing more than two feet ahead. The fog was just for effect since it dissipated the minute someone started down the boardwalk, turned right and followed a path into the Bayou.

Jimmy paid with pieces of eight for all of them and gallantly let the ladies take the lead. He wanted them ahead of him on the path. He had a plan.

"Mom, look at the alligators!" Outside it was late afternoon but inside, when the fog lifted, it was kept almost dark so that the eyes of the alligators glowed red.

Amy, Celeste and Maggie were having a wonderful time. Jimmy was biding his time.

Buck was terrified of the bayou and all the creepy, crawly things in the water. The minute he heard Amy talk about alligators he started to back up. Maybe this wasn't such a good idea. But it was too late.

Jimmy wanted to toss out some gold dust from his pocket but he knew his powers were dim to nothing over water.

Maggie heard his plea. She dropped back to join Jimmy. "I'll take care of this."

Suddenly the thick fog that had been at the entrance to the attraction enveloped Buck Boudreaux.

Amy and Celeste looked back but couldn't see anything.

Buck lost his balance in the fog and reached out for the railing. It had disappeared. They all heard a loud splash and a lot of terrible cursing.

Jimmy grinned. The alligators weren't real. They were made of rubber and fabric. Their movements were remote controlled, like the rubber snakes swimming around. They just looked scary. And the water was only ankle deep which made drowning impossible.

Jimmy patted Maggie's arm. "Good job!"

Amy was concerned until Jimmy told her he saw park personnel coming to the rescue and suggested they move quickly or they'd miss the boat that would take them on the bayou cruise.

Bt the time they finally exited the ride Buck was nowhere around.

Maggie said goodbye. She had some gift shopping to do.

Amy and Celeste were still talking about everything they had seen as they walked back to the Lodge.

It was late when they arrived home. Marie rushed to tell Amy and Celeste their ball gowns had arrived and Serena had just called and said she'd be over tomorrow to go to the Ball with them.

Amy touched Jimmy's arm.

He suddenly felt all dopey like his brother Danny when he was around her. "Tomorrow is your big day. I'll see you sometime in the morning."

"Okay." Amy thought about how much she'd miss him after Mardi Gras was over. It would be really great if they could find a reason to see him often.

Jimmy collected his things from the hall closet and suited up with his rocket pack.

Marie waited for him by the front door. "Can you be here tomorrow morning?

"Sure."

"Your costume will be here then. You do know you have a part in the Pirates Ball?"

"No, but it sounds like fun."

"Great. See you tomorrow."

"What part?"

"What?"

"What what, Marie? What part do I play? Geez!"

"I don't know. Someone called and said your beautiful costume would arrive in the morning."

"That is so exciting! I'll be here early."

Firing up the rockets he joyfully flung himself into the air for his flying trip back to the roof of the Golden Palace Hotel.

He couldn't wait to tell his brothers. He was positive he was going to be a duke or a prince at the Pirates Ball and walk next to Queen Amy while she waved her scepter to her loyal subjects. How fun! He would have to practice the royal wave.

Thankfully no one was around when he landed.

He made his way through the hotel lobby and the garden, filled with Mardi Gras tourists.

No one paid any attention to him wearing his rocket pack and dragging a banner behind him. This was the French Quarter. You could walk around in a costume and mask all year long and no one would even notice.

He was sad when he thought that after tomorrow he would no longer have a reason to hang out with Amy. She had been a lot of fun.

Bubba was furious with Buck when he heard what happened. The Boudreaux boys were turning into the laughing stock of the bayou. Bad enough he hadn't found a way to change them back to their human bodies but now a midget and a girl made them look like idiots.

He held an emergency meeting of the Boudreaux clan and made it very clear that there would be no more going off script until after the kidnaping. He sternly pointed out that Buck had decided to take his own course of action and look what happened...he failed. Bubba made everyone agree to stick to the plan he had made.

Seamus sat at the bar in Lafitte's Blacksmith Shop and used the bar phone, trying in vain to get a flight out of town back to Ireland. Nothing. If he was a piece of luggage he couldn't get mailed until after Mardi Gras. This was one time the entire city shut down.

Angus walked over. "No
luck?" "None."

"Maybe something will come up. Ye still have a return plane ticket."

"It's for a week from now!"

Angus laughed. "There are worse places to be stuck. People actually pay good money to come to Mardi Gras. Cheer up, Mate!"

"I guess."

"Look. I'll get ye a ticket to the Pirates Ball. Rent a tux and be in front of the Auditorium on Rampart tomorrow night. I'll meet ye there at seven. Don't forget, be there! It's hard to get an invitation."

"Thank ye, Angus. I wish I could go back to Ireland right now, but thank ye."

Angus smiled and walked to the end of the bar. It was starting to get busy again.

Jimmy couldn't hear his alarm clock ring the next morning. Before going to bed the night before had he tossed it into the closet. He smiled when he heard the clock banging in frustration against the closet door.

"Ha, ha, ha, you didn't get me today. This is a big day and I won't have you spoiling Mardi Gras for me. I'm going to be a duke in the Pirates Ball, so there!"

To avoid the huge crowds of tourists in the streets Jimmy once again went to the roof of the hotel, strapped on his rockets, and took off.

The entire way to the Lodge he thought about his role as a duke in the grand Pirates Ball. His name would be in headlines on the Ball program. He and Queen Amy would walk around the auditorium making small talk, and waving to all their loyal subjects. Everyone would be calling his name...Duke O'Brien! Or would it be Duke Jimmy? He was not up on what to call a duke or an earl. Anyway, he would soon find out.

Photographers would bump each other out of the way to take his picture. He would make the front page of the Dublin Times and that very famous magazine, Ireland Forever.

Duke O'Brien! He liked that a lot. It had a wonderful ring to it. The name flowed off his tongue like he'd always been a duke. Because of his new status he decided that when he next visited London he would graciously accept an invitation to tea with the Queen of England.

While visiting Buckingham Palace the Queen would mention that it would be a great honor to give him a royal title. And, of course, Duke O'Brien fit him so well. He would act surprised and be very humble and ...and...uh oh! Because he was not paying attention to his flying. He was heading full speed, head first, into the front yard of The Lodge. Doing some fast maneuvering he managed to flip over, slow way down, and land feet first on the lush green grass. Even so he bounced up and down a bit.

He arrived looking disheveled. Not at all like royalty!

Marie opened the door grinning. "Thank goodness you're here. I have your costume. LouLou said she was sure it would be a perfect fit."

Jimmy looked at something hanging on the coat rack by the door. It was something light blue and white, made of a shiny satin material. The costume had short pants, white leggings and a white satin shirt, with a baby blue fitted to the waist jacket, with balloon sleeves and huge shoulder pads. The whole thing was dotted with rhinestones. Rhinestones!

"What is that?"

"It's your page's costume."

"What is a page? And where is my duke's costume?"

"The page is the person who walks behind Queen Amy and makes sure no one steps on the train of her gown."

"You are kidding?" Jimmy was horrified. "I am going to be a duke. My costume has studs, diamonds, or at least Swarovski crystals, and made of heavy, embroidered silk damask—"

"---Who said anything about a duke?"

"I am not wearing that girly thing!"

Marie narrowed her eyes. "Yes, you are. There have always been pages in balls."

"And they have always been like five years old." "So?"

"So they were too young to know how ridiculous they looked wearing short satin pants and those leg thingies."

"You will wear this with a smile or I have not forgotten....shall I continue?"

"Uh."

"Well?"

"All right but this is blackmail."

"Don't forget to smile."

Jimmy plastered a big phony smile on his face and went in search of Amy.

Amy was in the dining room having a huge breakfast since alligator on a stick was all she ate since yesterday after the visit to LouLou.

"Jimmy!" Amy waved at him when he walked in. "Come and join me. There are such wonderful things to eat and hold your breath when you eat the powdered doughnuts." She laughed.

"I'm not hungry."

"Jimmy, what's wrong? You look awful."

"Oh, great, thanks."

"Ok...talk to me."

Jimmy struggled with not saying anything at all rather than end up sounding like a crybaby. He lost the struggle. "I have to wear some stupid page costume at the ball tonight and my job is to walk behind you and watch out for your dress."

"That does sound awful. Listen, I'd rather if you would walk next to me and we can laugh and talk about fun things and throw everyone the beads you bought for me. What do you say?"

"Okay." A small smile started and pretty soon he was laughing and in very good spirits. Amy was a great friend and he was sure no matter how stupid he looked in that jerky costume she'd make him feel okay about it.

Amy smiled. This was going to be a really great day.

"Grandmother should be here any minute now. I wanted her to come with us yesterday but she said she had tons of things to do but promised she'd spend today with us and she's bringing her gown for the ball."

After breakfast Celeste joined them in the parlor with a huge wood fire in the fireplace. Amy entertained everyone with stories about life in the orphanage.

It was late afternoon when Serena walked in to find they were all fast asleep.

Serena turned an antique crystal light fixture one of two flanking the fireplace mantel. She turned the light first to the right then to the left. A door in the bookcase opened.

Amy heard the creak of the secret door. She opened her eyes, wide with surprise. Serena motioned her to follow.

"What a beautiful room! I have never seen a secret room before." Amy whispered. "At my mother's house there was a secret staircase, with a passage to the street, beside the fireplace in my mother's room."

"I know. That room used to be for storage. I used to meet your grandfather there." Serena smiled. "There are things no one knew. Lafitte and I were married at the Cathedral by a visiting priest. Lafitte wanted to buy a perfect house for me so he left to collect his treasure hidden in the bayou. He never returned. The Claiborne's threw me out in the street with nothing but the clothes I was wearing. I had a bit in savings so I survived. I left New Orleans with not much more than my memories. I inherited powers from my parents. I knew a little but I had not perfected them as my brother, Marco, had done. I never talk about Marco. He lives in the French Quarter and has gone to the Dark Side. He has a huge following of people just as wicked as he is." Serena paused. Thinking about her evil brother was difficult. She continued, "I went to the Ozarks...to my Aunt Grace. She taught me everything about spells."

Serena urged Amy to sit beside her on the loveseat in the room. A fire blazed in the fireplace.

"Where is Aunt Grace now?"

Serena smiled. She met a gypsy on a trip to England. They travel the country in a caravan. Every now and then I get a letter from her. She is sublimely happy.

"Jimmy told me you created Pirate village."

"I did when I fell in love with Lafitte. At first it was a safe place. I used my gift to make it a magical place. Only pirates could come and go. It became an invisible means for him to get his smuggled goods from the Mississippi River through tunnels to a special back room at The Lafitte Blacksmith Shop. Later, when I returned with my son, I opened it up to not just pirates but to anyone with pirate blood."

"Why didn't he return?"

"I waited a long time. I was with child. I didn't want anyone's sympathy. I returned years later after I had amassed a fortune in real estate. I loved renovating properties. So I returned to the Quarter and built the Lodge, hoping Lafitte still might return. I heard his ship sunk in the Caribbean when he was returning to me."

"Then he is gone." Tears sprang to Amy's eyes.

"I had made him immortal. He decided not to find me. I was later told he was married and living somewhere in the Caribbean."

"But you were married to him!" Amy was astounded.

"He was Lafitte. He could do anything he wanted to do."

"And my father?"

"He chose to not return. I think he felt that without your mother he was lost in this world. You see no one knew you or your mother was still alive. We were told that all women and children were dead."

What Serena didn't say was that after the incident with the Boudreaux boys she had put a protective spell around her son. He might be immortal but until she put that special spell over him he could still get hurt. Not anymore. She sent a special plea to Philippe to return to her and his waiting family.

"I can't believe it's so late." Celeste stood in the doorway smiling. She looked around. "What a beautiful room."

"I had this built for Lafitte. He would laugh to hear me call him that. He always wanted to be called Lafitte. Did you know he is a great writer? And he has a wonderful sense of humor. When Governor Claiborne was alive he had posters put up all over New Orleans declaring a Five Hundred Dollar award for anyone capturing and delivering Jean Lafitte to the Sheriff of Orleans. Jean sat right down and wrote out his own poster declaring an award of One Thousand Five Hundred Dollars to be paid to anyone capturing Governor Claiborne and delivering him to Lafitte in the bayou! He had a great laugh over that."

"Oh, grandmother, I wish I had known him. I read that he was tall, very handsome and had the manners of a true gentleman."

"My darling girl, he was that and more." Serena smiled softly. "But now you must get dressed. It's already past five in the afternoon."

"Past five?" Amy was horrified. There was so much to do. She wanted to tell her mother everything her grandmother had told her but now was not the time.

"Afraid so. I came earlier but you were sleeping so peacefully. It will be a long night tonight."

They woke Jimmy and then the three ladies disappeared into Amy's bedroom where their dresses were hanging in a beautiful rosewood armoire.

Marie pointed out the powder room to Jimmy and handed him his costume. He dressed quickly keeping his eyes closed to make it less distressing and headed back to the parlor to wait for the ladies.

An hour later Amy came out wearing her gown, with a diamond and ruby tiara on her head. Jimmy could only stare in awe. She was truly the most beautiful Pirate Queen he'd ever seen. Her black hair was flowing over her shoulders and down her back. The diamonds in the tiara formed a Roman wreath with huge rubies here and there. She had a platinum scepter in her hand with a round tip made of diamonds and rubies.

Serena joined them wearing a LouLou creation, a long blue velvet gown with small diamond chips scattered about like stars twinkling in the night sky as she walked.

Celeste was last. She was wearing the Queen's gown she would have worn twenty years ago. It was a cream silk that clung to her beautiful figure. Tiny sapphires were scattered about the gown with the most concentrated at the bottom of her dress.

"Ladies?" Jimmy held the door open and they all walked out to the waiting limo.

Mickey opened the door and helped them inside.

Before Serena got in the limo she told Perkins to follow them. They were going to City Hall where they would be toasted by the Mayor. Amy would be given a gold key to the city in a small ceremony and then she would toast her Pirate King when the lead parade float, with the King sitting on his throne, stopped below the second floor balcony that faced the St. Charles Street entrance.

They had two special passes to park in the rear of City Hall. Mickey had a space directly in front of the rear door. Perkins had a space for Serena's car at the back of the parking lot.

"I'm not sure what I'm supposed to do but I'm sure it will come to me."

"In my day, " Celeste smiled, "The Queen and her court waited here for the parade to pass by and when the King's float stopped on the street below the Queen drank a toast to her King. Then the mayor gave her a token key to the city. Then the Queen got back in the limo and went to the Ball in the Auditorium on Rampart where she met up with her King. It's been the same since it first started."

"What happens at the Ball? Is there something special I have to do?"

"You take the arm of the mayor and walk around the Auditorium. Then he turns you over to your King and the two of you walk around waving to your loyal subjects while you throw out beads and doubloons." Celeste knew her daughter would know what to do when the time came.

"That's it?"

"That's it! Oh, then a select number of ladies sit in a special section where masked men, in costumes, come with a small gift and ask the ladies in the Call Out section to dance."

"That sounds like fun."

"Oh, it is!" Celeste thought back to the days when her parents took her to all the big balls.

They stopped talking while the aide to the mayor showed them where to sit in the front row of the viewing stands directly over the parade route.

Almost at once the parade of floats, called the Krewe of Pirates, started rolling. Amy toasted her King and received the gold key to the city of New Orleans. After the King's float left she watched the parade go by. One float was more magnificent than the next. The parade came to a halt as it sometimes happens.

Amy noticed a little girl on the street directly below the viewing stands. She was crying. Without giving it a thought Amy snatched up her long train and rushed down the side stairs to talk to the child.

"How can I help?"

"I lost my puppy. When I looked down Mindy was gone. This is her collar."

"Can I hold it?" Amy held out her hand.

The little girl nodded.

Amy took the collar and leash. She immediately felt the heat. The puppy was very close. She closed her eyes. She could see the puppy, terrified of the torches and loud music, slip out of her too loose collar and run under the float directly in front of them.

Lifting the skirt around the bottom of the float Amy called for Mindy in a very soft voice. The little puppy shot out at the sound of her name.

She put the collar on the little dog and brought the puppy back to the little girl.

"You found her! Thank you ever so much!"

"When you get home you have to adjust the collar so it fits well. It was too loose. Mindy slipped right out of it. Maybe it would be better if you didn't bring Mindy to anymore parades. I think she's terrified of the noise. And I think it would be better if you held Mindy for the rest of the time you're in the street."

"I will! I didn't know. Thank you. I can't believe you found her. You should be a detective and find lost puppies." The little girl laughed. "You would be a great detective."

"Not a bad idea." Amy patted Mindy on the head. The creak and groan of the floats alerted Amy that the parade was starting up again. "I have to go. Bye."

When she looked back the little girl was holding Mindy close to her heart.

What an interesting idea, she thought. She and Jimmy could start their own detective agency. And then she could see Jimmy all the time. Between her sense of touch and Jimmy's special powder they would do very well. The name "End of the French Quarter Detective Agency" popped into her head.

When Mickey got the note asking him if he could take the back stairs to the third floor and pick a box of fairly heavy Mardi Gras throws for Amy left outside the door to the bathroom, he didn't hesitate for a second.

He was delayed a bit trying to make his way through the "Throw me something, Mister" crowd. Finally he raced up the stairs and opened the door to the dark hallway on the third floor. He didn't see the person who hit him on the head. The last thing he saw was a cold blackness as he passed out.

He woke up groggy but alert enough to see a man snatch his chauffeur's hat off the floor and post something on the outside of the bathroom door. Mickey was bound and gagged but there was nothing wrong with his eyesight. The notice said "Out of order." No one would come looking for him until tomorrow. He struggled in vain. He prayed nothing would happen to Amy. The only consolation was that Serena was with her and that was one lady he wouldn't mess with.

Going back to her place on the balcony, Amy watched the rest of the Krewe of Pirates go by.

Amy was supposed to go alone in the limo but she really wanted her mom, her grandmother and Jimmy to go with her. They all piled into the limo and wondered where Mickey was. Their driver was missing. But they soon forgot that fact since they had so much to talk about. Amy told Jimmy about the idea for the detective agency. He liked the idea, too.

Just about the time Amy was going to mention something about Mickey being missing the driver's door of the limo opened and someone got in. Amy wondered who this driver was because the he made a point of locking the doors. Mickey would have turned to say hello first.

CHAPTER TWELVE

The Lafitte Family Reunites At The Ghost Ball

Beau didn't like the fact that Amy wasn't alone in the back of the limo. There were two other ladies, probably maids in the court and a little page. He'd been to enough Mardi Gras balls to know that a page was usually a little kid and no threat at all.

Everything happened so fast that Bubba, all his Cajun rat brothers and cousin Buck, who were hiding in and around trash cans fifty feet away, were watching the unfolding scene with horror, helpless to do anything. They knew what Serena would do to them if they were caught.

Beau thought he was on top of the world. He flipped the intercom and said in a menacing tone of voice, "I control the door locks. You can't escape. This is a kidnaping. I only want Amy so at some point I'll drop off you two other girls and the kid."

Serena laughed out loud. With a twist of her wrist and a snap of her fingers she turned Beau into a Cajun rat in a locked cage on the front seat. With another twist of her wrist the rest of the Boudreaux clan appeared in the same cage.

"Jimmy, go get Mickey. You'll find him tied up in the bathroom on the third floor."

"Yes, ma'am!" Jimmy hopped out of the limo but not before having the last laugh at the caged Cajun rat in the front seat. "Hey, Beau, stupid idiot, I'm not a kid, either."

In no time Jimmy returned with Mickey. With Perkins' help, they transferred the cage with the rats to the trunk of the limo.

Serena had a quiet conversation with Mickey. She told him she trusted him with the cargo in the trunk but she would be back in a few hours to pick it up.

Serena took Amy's hand. "My darling girl, there is something I have to do. I will join you and your Mom in the Auditorium. I probably won't be back for a while. Wait for me."

"Of course. Thank you, Grandmother. You saved my life."

Serena smiled. "I'll never let anything happen to you or your Mom. Now go with Mickey and I'll see you later."

She watched Mickey take away her precious granddaughter. She just had one little thing to do.

Seamus checked his watch again. It was six-thirty. People, dressed in fantastic costumes, were rushing into the Auditorium, tickets in hand. A long, sleek black car pulled up. A power window went down and a woman said his name. Seamus stopped pacing and turned to look into the open window.

"I heard you wanted to go back to Ireland tonight and there are no flights available."

"I don't recall meeting ye before."

"We have a friend in common...Angus. He mentioned it. I have a private jet if you're interested in a ride."

"Ye know Angus?"

"Call him. He has his cell phone with him. Tell him Serena is taking you to Dublin."

"I really do want to go home." That seemed to settle things.

Seamus called his friend.

Angus laughed and told him if he was with Serena he was in good hands. Go. He'd gather his things and send them by mail.

The car door opened and Seamus got inside. "Thank ye!"

Polly, the parrot, flew in through the open window and landed on the seat next to Serena like it was the most natural thing in the world. "Hi, ho, just got your message. Where are we going?"

Before Seamus had a chance to ask if that was really a talking parrot he fell sound asleep with a little help from Serena, which was just as well, fewer questions to answer.

"We're going to London."

"Oh, thank you, thank you!" Polly was so excited she squawked, which she hardly every did, and beat her wings in joy. Parrot feathers flew all over the place. She bet she was going to be the first Mexican jungle parrot that flew over Big Ben. It took a while for her to calm down.

Perkins drove the car to a dark part of the parking lot behind the Auditorium. No one was around. Everyone was inside as the Pirates Ball had already started.

In seconds the car changed into a carriage that shot through the sky faster than a 747.

Seamus woke up in the same black car he had gotten into earlier in the evening only now they were somewhere in London and it was raining!

"I will drop you off outside of Dublin but first I have one stop to make." Seamus noticed a lovely jungle parrot in a cage. "Can that parrot talk?".

Polly thought she'd tease him a bit and said "Stupid, parrots can't talk!"

Serena admonished her. "Stop that."

Answering him she said, "That's Polly. She's along for the ride."

They pulled up in front of a small office building in a deserted part of London. Paint peeling off the wood siding made it look abandoned. Serena was not fooled. This place housed her enemy, Captain Murphy, the man responsible for sinking his own ship for the insurance money. In the water, adrift, her precious grandchild, Amy, was left on the doorstep of an orphanage for thirteen years and her daughter-in-law believed her entire family had died, along with everyone else on the ship. All this because of the greed of one man, Captain Murphy. He was long overdue for what Serena had in mind for him. And it wasn't going to be very nice.

"We're here. Seamus, wait in the car. Believe me, I won't be long."

Polly hopped in the cage and Serena covered it with a cloth. "Ready, Polly?"

"Ready, Teddy."

"Where do you get stuff like that?" "TV."

"It figures."

Serena walked into the coolness of the entryway and checked the very short list of offices. She saw Captain

Murphy had his office right down the hall. Very convenient, she thought.

"Showtime, Polly."

She opened the door to Office 101 and walked in.

A young girl was sitting at a reception desk. There were a few chairs scattered around the austere office. Serena thought Murphy certainly had not used his ill gotten gains from sinking his own ship for the comfort of his visitors.

"Hello. I have an Amazonian parrot for Captain Murphy."

Polly wanted to scream "Mexican parrot, please!" but kept her beak shut before Serena changed her back into the young girl from Mexico, broke and out of a visa, who begged Serena to make her into a beautiful parrot who could talk and fly.

"He was just saying the other day he'd love to have a parrot. Kind of a sea captain thing I guess."

Serena moved the curtain aside to show her. "Polly, say hello to the pretty lady."

"Hello, pretty lady." Polly squawked.

The young girl was enchanted.

"Go right in. He's not busy."

Serena opened the door and walked in. She was careful to shut it behind her.

Captain Murphy, who was without manners, didn't bother to get up. She set the cage on his huge desk.

"I was just thinking about getting a parrot the other day."

"Really?" Serena took the cover off the cage. "May I?" Indicating she wanted to open the cage door.

"Of course but my window is open."

"She won't fly out. She's very obedient."

"I like that!"

"And she can talk."

"I don't believe it!"

"Ask her something."

"Okay. What did I have for breakfast this morning?"

The parrot laughed. "Oh, that's easy. You had a fried egg sandwich and chocolate milk."

"Why I'll be! How did you know that?" He totally ignored the fact that he was talking to a parrot.

Polly hopped out of the cage and fluttered to the top of a file cabinet. "Well....you have egg yolk dribbled on your vest which can only come from eating a fried egg sandwich that you just finished right before we came in, and there is a bit of chocolate milk on your upper lip."

Captain Murphy looked at his vest and quickly wiped away the egg yolk and dabbed at his mouth.

"I have to have that bird. I've never seen a parrot like that." He stood up and leaned his hands on the desk. "How much do you want? Name your price!'

"There are some things you, Captain Murphy, can't buy, even with all the insurance money you got from sinking, The Ella Mae."

Narrowing his eyes, he growled, "Why don't we talk about this?"

He started moving his hand slowly towards a gun in the open desk drawer to his right.

With a twist of her wrist and a snap of her fingers Captain Murphy was now an Irish rat in a cage on his desk.

The cage door slammed shut. Captain Murphy was not able to open his mouth to scream no matter how hard he tried.

Serena placed the cover over the cage. "Polly, out the window, off you go. Meet us in the meadow where we started. You still have the coordinates?"

"Of course! I'll be there. See you soon." Polly flew out the window.

Serena opened the door and walked into the office. "He didn't want the lovely parrot and he said not to bother him for the rest of the day. Take the afternoon off, he said."

"Don't have to tell me twice. I'll lock up behind you."

The two women went into the hallway. "When he says that he means private business is coming to visit and I have to leave. I get lots of early afternoons off."

I bet, Serena thought, with a smile, and got into her waiting car.

"Perkins, back to the field." The car drove off.

Serena turned to Seamus. "We are picking up Polly and then we'll drop you off in Ireland. But first, an ID check."

Serena took the cover off the cage.

Seamus was astounded to see Captain Murphy's face on a rat body. "That's him, alright. And now he's an Irish rat! I'd say it's fits him just fine."

"He'll have a grand time with the Cajun rats, don't you think?" Serena smiled.

"From what I learned the Cajuns hate the Irish."

"Yes, and there are many Cajun rats and only one Irish rat. Sad, isn't it?" Serena laughed. She wasn't one bit sad.

From now on this evil man was going to live a nightmare of her creation.

Seamus laughed. He was free at last. Captain Murphy can't harm his family now. And his brother can return home.

Serena covered the cage.

The traffic was heavy but Perkins was originally from London so he knew his way around with ease.

Finally, they arrived back at the meadow.

"Do you think Polly will find us?" Seamus looked out the window.

"Of course she'll find us. Polly had the highest score in her navigation class at Tulane."

"She took a navigation class?"

"What can I say...she loves to learn."

Polly, waiting for them, swooped down from the sky and landed on the seat next to Serena.

"Ok, I am so excited! So excited! Big surprise I have to tell you! I saw the Queen and Kate walking in the garden at the Castle. They were laughing together. They were ever so happy! This was the best day of my life. I saw Big Ben and the Savoy Hotel and everything! And did I mention the Queen and Kate!"

"Polly, you're not going to turn into a name dropping parrot, I hope."

Polly laughed. "I don't think so."

Serena leaned forward in her seat. "Perkins, find a meadow on the outskirts of Dublin."

With a twist of her wrist and a snap of her fingers the car changed into a flying carriage.

London was soon behind them as they hugged the coast headed for Ireland.

They landed in an isolated field and Seamus got out. "I can make my way home from here. For the first time I'm free of that horrible man."

"When Murphy sank his ship I almost lost my precious granddaughter that night in the violent seas. So believe me when I say you will never see Captain Murphy again and his fate, in my hands, is more horrible than anything you can even imagine. Go find your brother in exile and bring him home. Your mother has missed him dearly."

Seamus watched the carriage rise in the sky and disappear leaving only a trail of wispy cloud behind. He could never tell anyone about this. Who would believe him anyway!

In a short while the carriage landed in the parking lot of the Auditorium.

Everyone was still at the Pirates Ball so their arrival was unseen except for Mickey who had been waiting for Serena to return.

"Polly, go home."

Polly happily flew out the window. She couldn't wait to tell Annie all about London and seeing the Queen and everything.

Mickey and Perkins transferred the large cage holding all the Cajun rats from Mickey's trunk, adding the new addition of Captain Murphy, they strapped the lot to the back of the carriage.

Mickey waved goodbye and returned with his limo to the front of the Auditorium.

The carriage lifted in the air and in a flash they were flying to Rat Island, an acre of sharp glass shards on a small beach with scrub bushes all over. It's nothing like a tropical island in travel brochures. There is water and some almost inedible fruit trees. Most of the available food are worms under rocks or termites and ants under tree bark. Mostly disgusting, it's surrounded by hungry sharks, making escape impossible. There wasn't a rat in the group that could swim far enough to reach freedom anyway.

The carriage hovered over the island. Before she opened the cage doors and dumped all the rats onto the glass sharp sandy beach she lifted the glass window behind her and introduced the Irish rat to the group.

"You Cajun rats, listen up. This new rat is Murphy, he's Irish. Because of Murphy you all have come to this end. I hope you treat this Irish rat accordingly."

She could hear the gnashing of teeth and snarls from the Cajun bunch.

Serena smiled. She gave Captain Murphy his voice back and made the Irish rat immortal.

The last thing she heard as she dumped them onto the bleak beach was the screams of Captain Murphy. He was coming to the realization that he couldn't even pray that death would come swiftly because his torture was for eternity.

"Perkins, back to the Auditorium!"

"She planned on returning, after a while, to bring the Boudreax boys back to the French Quarter and restoring them to their human bodies. But first she was going to leave them on the island, giving them time to have a big attitude change.

The carriage landed quietly in a secluded spot, next to thick hedge, in the parking lot behind the Auditorium where it changed back into a sleek black sedan.

Perkins dropped Serena off in front of the Auditorium. During the carriage ride back she had changed into the blue silk velvet gown LouLou had made for her. Diamonds, like tiny stars embedded in the bottom of the long gown, glistened as she walked.

She easily found her way to the call out section just as the dances were about to begin.

"Oh Grandmother, I am having so much fun. This is a wonderful night!" For a second she thought about her Dad and a shadow of sadness flitted across her eyes. "Well...I mean..."

"I know, Amy." Serena touched her hand.

Celeste joined them. "The rest rooms are packed. Serena, I'm so happy to see you but you missed Amy in her walkabout. I did notice there was someone photographing everything, so we can watch it later."

"I had something very important to do or I would have been here." Serena watched three men headed their way. "Look, I think we are about to have our first call outs."

Even though they had on masks Amy recognized them as the pirates from Treasure Island.

They formally handed identical small boxes to each of the three ladies. Then with a bow they extended their hands for a dance. Amy followed the lead of the ladies around her and left the gift unopened on her chair.

Without a word they whirled around the dance floor. When it was over they returned the ladies to their seats and bowed before leaving.

Amy eagerly opened her gift. A piece of very old parchment was inside. Intrigued she unfurled the paper proclamation. It read

You are invited to a Ghost Ball. Leave now. Go to the roof of The Golden Palace Hotel and show your invitation. You will ascend into the sky by a glass enclosed elevator. You must hurry.

Looking up Amy realized her mother and grandmother both had the same invitation. "Grandmother, do you know what this is?"

"Yes. This is an honor. They hold a Ghost Ball rarely and on the spur of the moment. The guests are all the most famous Pirates. They are all ghosts. You might see this only once in your lifetime. We must go immediately."

"What about Jimmy?" Amy nodded to the little guy who was snoring in his seat.

"Good grief!" Serena laughed. "Wake him up. The last time they had a Ghost Ball was over one hundred years ago. I certainly don't want to listen to him complaining that he missed the Ball."

Amy gently touched his shoulder. "Jimmy, I'm going to a Ghost Ball. Want to come?"

He leaped up like he hadn't been sound asleep only three seconds ago.

Amy had never seen him move so fast. She turned to Serena. "He doesn't have an invitation. What do we do?"

Serena thought for a second. "No, but he's got a job. Jimmy act like a page."

Jimmy finally did his job making sure that no one stepped on Amy's dress.

Perkins was waiting in front of the Auditorium. They got into the black car, drove to the back of the building and changed into the carriage. With the Mardi Gras revelers in the street this was the only way to go.

The carriage gently touched down on the rooftop of the hotel.

Someone opened the carriage door and asked for their invitations.

Once they showed their passes they were allowed into a glass elevator. They ascended into the rarified air of the night sky at a dizzy speed. The lights of the French Quarter disappeared below them. Amy was intrigued with this method of transport. She couldn't find any seams in the glass. It was so incredibly clear the stars looked so close she felt she could reach out and touch them. They kept going higher and higher.

Each of the women was lost in their own thoughts. Celeste had been unusually quiet. If only Philippe could be here to see his lovely daughter, Queen of the Pirates' Ball. She knew if she said even one word she'd burst into tears.

The elevator finally slowed and came to a stop. The doors opened with a sigh and they walked into a huge glass ballroom. Even the ceiling was glass.

A large orchestra was on the far side of the room.

Costumed, masked figures whirled around the dance floor to a Strauss Waltz. The women wore elaborate ball gowns made of vibrant colored silk, satin and velvet. One more beautiful than the next.

Everyone recognized the new arrivals, the only non ghosts in the room.

Instantly an usher was at their side leading them to a slightly raised platform along one wall where they could see everything.

Jimmy huddled behind Amy's dress. He was terrified and excited at the same time.

"Look!" Amy tugged on Jimmy's puffy shoulder pad. "That's Blackbeard!"

There was no mistaking Edward Teach, known to everyone as Blackbeard. He was easily close to seven feet tall with a massive girth, wild unkept jet black hair and a long jet black bushy beard woven with sparklers. Every now and again he set one of them ablaze making his beard look like it was on fire.

Jimmy laughed. "In the Pirate Treasure Game he stands at the wheel of his ship, the Queen Anne's Revenge, and when he lights up his beard it's so terrifying that the other ship's crew jumps in the water rather than being attacked by the devil himself."

Serena smiled. "He's really a sweet man. I'll introduce you later. Amy, Blackbeard or Edward Teach, his real name, is one of your relatives."

"How exciting!"

"He sent his daughter, Sofia, to attend the social season in New Orleans. She was a beautiful girl and caught the attention of Governor Claiborne's youngest son. They fell madly in love and married over the violent objection of both Teach and Claiborne. But there was little either of the powerful men could do since a visiting priest at the Cathedral, not knowing the situation, married them himself."

They watched Blackbeard dance with every beautiful female ghost in the room.

Every famous pirate was here, as a ghost, of course.

"I wish this Ball could go on forever." Amy took off her shoes to give her feet a rest from all the dancing.

"The young do think that way. Sadly it ends at midnight." Serena watched the elevator doors. If it was going to happen it had to be soon.

"Like Cinderella?"

"Yes, but our carriage will still be

there." "I wish—"

"I know and I tried."

At precisely one minute to midnight, the glass elevator doors opened.

The sound caught everyone's attention, looking to see who the late arrivals were.

A huge gasp went up from the ballroom.

Who didn't recognize the most famous pirate of them all?

The crowd parted making a path directly to Serena, Celeste and Amy.

Two men walked across the ballroom side by side. There was no mistaking that they were father and son since Jean Lafitte and his son Philippe looked so much alike. Both were well over six feet tall, dressed all in black, fair complexions, black silky hair that fell over their foreheads in the same way that made every woman they passed want to tuck it back and catch their attention but their hearts were already taken long ago by the women just steps away. Lafitte twirled Serena in the air.

Philippe hugged Celeste and Amy close to his heart, never to let them go again. He recognized Amy immediately. She was the image of her mother.

"Papa, I missed you so much. I'm so happy you're here."

"I was told no one survived. They found the children's boat empty. My heart broke. I thought I had lost you and your mother forever."

Amy was speechless in her happiness. All she wanted to do was hold onto them and never let them go.

Lafitte pulled a black velvet box out of his pocket. "I came back for you but they told me you were gone. They told me you married and moved to Europe."

"How could I do that? I was married to you. It was you I loved." Lafitte took her hand in his. "I was seeking my treasure. The hurricane made it impossible to find. I didn't want to come back until I could buy you a house, give you everything."

"I didn't need all that, Lafitte. I only needed you. But my darling, you are here now and I see providence put you in the same elevator with our son."

"I knew him at once. We need time now to get to know one another. First I have something for you that I've carried with me a long time."

He went down on one knee and pulled a dark blue velvet box out of his pocket. He had kept the magnificent diamond ring prisoner for so long, waiting until he was once again with the only woman he had ever married and ever loved that when he opened the lid the diamond threw out fireworks of color and rainbows that shot into the night sky right through the glass ceiling.

Tourists and residents in the French Quarter, including the entire city of New Orleans, would forever talk about the most incredible fireworks display of all time filling the sky just before midnight on this Mardi Gras Day.

Lafitte slipped the ring on Serena's hand. "Marry me again!"

Amy turned to Jimmy who stood there transfixed.

"Oh, Jimmy, this is the happiest day of my life. So many wonderful things have happened these past few weeks. I have a family and you, my good friend. So now that everyone is back together let's talk about *The End of the French Quarter Detective Agency.* This story can't possible end now!"

NOT THE END, JUST THE BEGINNING

Here's a little bit of the exciting sequel to "Amy, Queen of the Pirates Ball"

"Pirate Amy and The French Quarter Detective
Agency
Case# 1: The Missing Treasure Map"

Chapter One
Amy And Jimmy Start A Detective Agency

The day after Mardi Gras, in the French Quarter, is almost as noisy as the night before only it's not serious party goers making all the noise, it's heavy duty cleaning trucks.

Just before dawn they sweep through the deserted streets pushing broken Hurricane glasses, torn plastic beer cups, smashed Mardi Gras beads and containers of to-go Red Beans and Rice, Jambalaya, Gumbo and broken sticks that once held grilled alligator tail meat.

This molten, broken mixture is swept to the curbs and then sucked into giant holding tanks later to be deposited at city dump sites.

A few hours later tourists stumble from their hotels in the French Quarter, amazed at the clean streets beneath their feet. Taxi cabs wait patiently to take their fares on an expensive trip to the airport, fifteen miles from the city center.

Two Months Later

The Lafitte family is back from their world cruise. The minute Amy returned she called Jimmy. She couldn't wait to tell him all the news and talk about their new business venture.

The next morning Amy woke up...late. Leaping out of bed she dressed quickly in navy sweats.

Last night they had spoken briefly about the detective agency but they needed to finalize the details. She told

Jimmy to come by for breakfast, that now qualified for lunch.

She found him in the small cozy library. There was a huge wood fire blazing.

"Ah, the world traveler is back!"

"Jimmy! We had a really great adventure!"

"And thank you for all the postcards. I felt like I was there, too."

"I wish you had been." She smiled at her friend. She had missed him terribly. "We took a river cruise on the Thames. Everyone we met told Lafitte, he definitely wants everyone to call him Lafitte, anyway everyone told him looked like the real thing. He said he knew that and gets a lot of work playing the pirate, Jean Lafitte."

Jimmy smiled. "That must have been something to see. How about your Grandmother? Until just a few weeks ago she never left her house in Pirate Village and now she's a world traveler."

"Granny was very good. Oh, by the way, she likes to be called Granny. Anyway, she only did one little thing. Lafitte wanted beignets with his afternoon tea so she made them appear. Everyone around our table was really amazed." Amy laughed. "Everyone except our group, of course. Granny said she had bought them in London but couldn't remember where. Must be old age, she said, which was very funny since she much be about three hundred years old."

"She doesn't look a day over two hundred and for Heaven's sake don't tell her I said that!"

"You know we took Polly Parrot with us! She was over the top being in London again. Annie was ever so put out but Granny said Annie would have to give up her tail. A dog with a monkey tail would attract too much attention. No way was she doing that! Annie was pouting big time so Granny had to promise Annie she could fly like Polly when we got back."

"Does she fly now?" Jimmy grinned trying to imagine the little black and white Jack Russell Terrier with wings.

"NO! Even Annie thought she looked just <u>too</u> weird with wings!"

"Now on to business. I have been busy since we talked last night."

"Tell me! Tell me! Wait. Let me get us some tea." Amy clapped her hands and rushed out of the room.

Amy returned from the dining room with a tray bearing cups of tea, and a plate of biscuits that she handed to Jimmy. He was busy writing copious notes about something that held his interest.

She plopped down in a leather overstuffed chair. "So, what's up?"

Jimmy closed the notebook with a snap. "Do you know what we need?"

"An ottoman for my feet!" Amy lifted her feet in the air.

"Oh, let me just rush to put that on the list with the thousand other things starting with a problem to solve and paying clients for our new business. Also someone to answer the phones would be nice."

"Don't forget an office with our names on the door." Amy smiled. No one made her laugh like her good friend.

"I think I solved that one. This morning on my way over here I saw Suzie putting a For Rent sign in the window of The Sweet Shop."

"What a great location." Amy sat forward in her chair.

"I thought so, too, so I went in and asked her if she would hold it until I talked to you, but I said I was sure you would be thrilled. I did mention were starting a detective agency. And of course she agreed and took the For Rent sign down immediately."

"Wonderful! I believe in getting the word out right away. And it has that store room with the brick wall."

"We'll have lots of clients from Pirates Village, too."

"Jimmy, let's call her."

"Do you still have her number at the Sweet Shop?"

"I do...somewhere." Amy rushed out of the room. She returned shortly waving a piece of paper.

Jimmy dialed the number. "Suzie, hi, we're definitely taking the shop. We'll be there shortly to sign the lease."

He answered yes a few time and then hung up. "I have good news, too."

"What did she say?"

"She said that two sisters, Lynne and Gayle, they live in the Garden District, anyway they stopped by on their way back from Cafe du Monde and noticed the sign was out of the window. Suzie told them the shop was going to be leased to a Detective Agency. They said that just that morning they had been talking about finding a detective agency to locate a relative who is missing along with a family heirloom...a treasure map. Amy, me dear, we might have our first client!"

To Be Continued

Made in the USA
Monee, IL
24 July 2022

10270747R00152